The bouqu...

She smiled as ...
blurring with tears as she read it.

*For my new mommy on her first Mother's Day. Love,
Oliver xoxo.*

She looked at Ryan. "Crayon?"

"Oliver doesn't yet have the dexterity to hold a
pen." She shot him a look and he said, "Okay, but
he wrote on the back."

She saw the blue scribble there.

She kissed the little boy on the cheek. "Thank you
for the pretty flowers, Oliver."

"Shouldn't I get a thank-you, too?" Ryan asked.

"Thank you," she said.

His brows lifted. "What about a kiss for me?"

She took a step closer and let her gaze settle on
his lips. She'd thought about Oliver's mom all day,
how much she admired her friend's willingness to
go after what she wanted. She wished she could be
that fearless and reach for what *she* wanted.

Ryan was so close, all she had to do was rise up on
her toes and brush her lips against his. Then take
his hand and lead him to her bedroom.

Could she be fearless enough to do it?

**THOSE ENGAGING GARRETTS!:
The Carolina Cousins**

Dear Reader,

Ryan Garrett is charming and easygoing;
Harper Ross is single-minded and ambitious. They
don't have much in common—in fact, they don't
particularly even like one another. But when a tragic
accident results in Ryan and Harper becoming joint
guardians of an orphaned baby boy, they have no
choice but to put aside their personal differences
and work together.

The stakes are raised further when their
guardianship is challenged. Ryan's vow to fight for
custody dispels Harper's laid-back image of him;
her own willingness to do the same proves she isn't
as self-centered as he believed. So maybe they're
not as different as they think—and maybe, on their
journey toward discovering the true meaning of
family, they'll realize that they need one another as
much as baby Oliver needs both of them.

I hope you enjoy their story!

Happy reading,

Brenda Harlen

PS. Stay tuned for the next installment of
Those Engaging Garretts! and see how sexy
bartender Marco Palermo convinces beautiful
heiress Jordyn Garrett that forever is the right path
for them!

A Forever Kind
of Family

———

Brenda Harlen

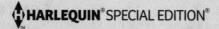

Recycling programs for this product may not exist in your area.

ISBN-13: 978-0-373-65885-5

A Forever Kind of Family

Copyright © 2015 by Brenda Harlen

Printed in U.S.A.

www.Harlequin.com

Brenda Harlen is a former attorney who once had the privilege of appearing before the Supreme Court of Canada. The practice of law taught her a lot about the world and reinforced her determination to become a writer—because in fiction, she could promise a happy ending! Now she is an award-winning, national bestselling author of more than thirty titles for Harlequin. You can keep up-to-date with Brenda on Facebook and Twitter or through her website, brendaharlen.com.

Books by Brenda Harlen

Harlequin Special Edition

Those Engaging Garretts!

The Daddy Wish
A Wife for One Year
The Single Dad's Second Chance
A Very Special Delivery
His Long-Lost Family
From Neighbors...to Newlyweds?

Montana Mavericks: 20 Years in the Saddle!

The Maverick's Thanksgiving Baby

Montana Mavericks: Rust Creek Cowboys

A Maverick under the Mistletoe

Montana Mavericks: Back in the Saddle

The Maverick's Ready-Made Family

Reigning Men

Royal Holiday Bride
Prince Daddy & the Nanny

Visit the Author Profile page at Harlequin.com for more titles.

One of the best things about setting this book in the fictional town of Charisma, North Carolina, was that it gave me an excuse to visit that beautiful state and some wonderful friends who call it home.

In particular, I would like to dedicate this book to the lovely and immensely talented Virginia Kantra, with much appreciation for carving time out of her busy schedule to have lunch with me...
which somehow extended to dinner...
and I think there might have been wine...

Chapter One

The baby was crying.

Harper Ross jolted awake, her heart pounding and her throat aching.

After eighteen days—and eighteen nights—she should have been accustomed to Oliver's middle-of-the-night outbursts, but she wasn't. By this time, she'd expected to feel more comfortable with the baby and more confident about her ability to care for him, but she didn't.

As the assistant producer of an award-winning television show, she wasn't just competent but confident. When she was in the studio, she was in charge and in control. When she was with her best friend's orphaned little boy, though, she felt completely helpless.

She didn't know what to do for him, how to console him—or if anything could. She was completely out of her element with the child. When she'd learned that she was now responsible for sixteen-month-old Oliver—she'd panicked.

She didn't know the first thing about caring for a child. She didn't know what to feed him, when to put him to bed or even how to change a diaper.

Thankfully, she knew how to research, and the internet was overflowing with information—including step-by-step video demonstrations of diaper changing. But there was still so much she didn't know, and every free minute she had, she spent reading childcare manuals and psychology textbooks.

She wouldn't have minded the steep learning curve so much except that her co-guardian—Ryan Garrett—had stepped into his role with no apparent difficulty, his ease with the child highlighting her own ineptitude. And although Ryan usually dealt with Oliver's middle-of-the-night demands, he didn't seem to be responding tonight.

She and Ryan had given up their respective apartments and moved into Melissa and Darren Cannon's house so that Oliver would be able to stay in familiar surroundings, but she knew that nothing could ease the loss of his parents.

She drew in a slow deep breath and pushed her legs over the edge of the mattress, swallowing around the lump in her throat. Her best friend's baby needed so much more than she could give him, but she was trying. Of course, she might be more successful if she could get more than a few hours of uninterrupted sleep in any given night, but so far that hadn't happened.

Oliver had apparently started sleeping through the night when he was five months old, but he hadn't done so even once since the accident. According to Ryan's mom, who had become their go-to source for all child-related questions, his nighttime waking was neither surprising nor cause for concern. His life and his routines had been disrupted and it was reasonable that he would be upset and confused. Harper's understanding of that didn't make her any less cranky.

And as the baby continued to cry, his sobs punctuated with heartfelt entreaties for "Ma-ma-ma-ma-ma," she wanted to cry right along with him. Instead she padded across the hall.

Other than the soft glow of the night-light that emanated from the baby's room, the hall was in complete darkness. She had no concept of time: how long she'd been sleeping or—

The unfinished thought was snatched from her brain along with the air from her lungs when she collided with a wall.

Not a real wall, but the wall of Ryan Garrett's chest.

Solid, strong, naked.

And wet.

His hands, strong and steady, caught her hips as she stumbled backward. She felt the imprint of every finger through the whisper-thin cotton of her boxer-short pajama bottoms, and the heat of his touch made her skin tingle and her pulse race in a way she hadn't experienced in a very long time—and definitely didn't want to be experiencing now.

She sucked in a breath and inhaled the clean, fresh scent of a man just out of the shower. Which explained why he was wet—but not why he was wandering around the house half-dressed.

"I just turned off the shower when I heard Oliver crying," he responded to her unspoken question. "I was trying to get to him before he woke you up."

"Too late." She winced as the baby's cries hit the next decibel range. "So maybe you could take the time now to put some clothes on?"

Her tone was sharper than she'd intended, but she didn't

apologize for snapping at him. She knew it wasn't his fault that the child's cries had awakened her, but she was half-asleep and his half-naked torso was waking up parts of her that she didn't want awakened, so she wasn't in a mood to be fair.

"I'm wearing pants," he said, following her into the baby's room. And though it was too dark for her to see the sexy half smile on his face, she could hear it in his voice. "In fact, I put them on just for you."

As if pajama bottoms sitting low on his hips could be classified as pants.

The man knew how attractive he was. After all, he was a Garrett, and it wasn't a hardship to look at any one of them. To describe Ryan as tall, dark and handsome would be accurate but completely inadequate. Those complimentary but generic words didn't begin to do him justice. He was at least six-foot-two, because he towered over her own five-six frame even when she was wearing heels. His hair was thick and soft and the color of dark roasted coffee beans; his brows were the same shade, straight and thick over eyes that were probably noted as hazel on his driver's license but were actually mossy green with flecks of golden amber. His jaw was strong and square and often covered with stubble. She didn't usually like the unshaven look that seemed to be in vogue these days but couldn't deny that it suited him, somehow increasing rather than lessening his appeal.

But Harper had grown up surrounded by beautiful people, so she wasn't readily enamored of a handsome face or an appealing physique—and Ryan Garrett had been blessed with both. Far more dangerous, at least to her way of thinking, was the quick mind and easy smile that added to the package. As if that wasn't enough to stack the odds in his favor, he was also friendly and charming and kind. And if her brain had been more awake than asleep, she would have spun on her heel and gone back to her own bed. Instead she followed him into the baby's room.

She turned on the lamp beside the rocking chair while he went directly to the crib and lifted Oliver into his arms. The baby's heart-wrenching cries immediately ebbed to shuddery sobs as he snuggled against Ryan's strong chest.

Harper hovered a few feet away, feeling useless and ineffectual as she watched him soothe the distressed child. His voice was low and even, and the sexy timbre was enough to stir the blood in her veins.

She knew only too well how it would feel to be cradled in his strong embrace, to lay her cheek on his chest and feel the beating of his heart. She knew because she'd spent one incredibly magical night in his arms—then the sun had come up, bringing not just morning but the harshness of reality.

"What's wrong, buddy?" Ryan crooned to Oliver softly. "Are you wet? Hungry?" He patted the baby's bottom. "Yep—a diaper change is definitely in order."

She watched him work, noting how Ryan held Oliver in place on the changing table with one hand splayed on the boy's tummy while he rummaged on the shelf beneath for a clean diaper. He made it look so effortless and easy, while she worked up a sweat trying to prevent the little guy from wriggling off the edge whenever she attempted the task. Which was, admittedly, not nearly as often as Ryan did.

Over the past two and a half weeks, they'd started to establish a routine. He took care of Oliver in the mornings while she was at work, and when she got home from the studio, he would go into his office for a few hours. They hadn't created a specific schedule for grocery shopping or laundry yet, but Harper was pretty sure that, in the past week, Ryan had done the bulk of those chores, too. She usually started dinner before he got home, and after they finished eating, they worked together to clean up, followed by bath time for the baby. But when it was Oliver's bedtime, he'd made it clear early on that he preferred falling asleep in Harper's arms.

Ryan glanced over his shoulder at her now as he finished fastening the tabs on the diaper. "Go back to bed, Harper. I've got him."

Since her alarm would be going off at 4:45 a.m., she wanted to do exactly that. When she'd gone back to work a few days after the funeral, Ryan had offered to be the one to get up in the night with Oliver so that she could sleep through. It wasn't his fault that she heard every sound that emanated from Oliver's room, across the hall from her own.

Thankfully, she worked behind the scenes at *Coffee Time with Caroline*, Charisma's most popular morning news show, so the dark circles under her eyes weren't as much a problem as the fog that seemed to have enveloped her brain. And that fog was definitely a problem.

"Do you want me to get him a drink?" she asked as Ryan zipped up Oliver's sleeper.

"I can manage," he assured her. "Go get some sleep."

Just as she decided that she would, Oliver—now clean and dry—stretched his arms out toward her. "Up."

Ryan deftly scooped him up in one arm. "I've got you, buddy."

The little boy shook his head, reaching for Harper. "Up."

"Harper has to go night-night, just like you," Ryan said.

"Up," Oliver insisted.

He looked at her questioningly.

She shrugged. "I've got breasts."

She'd spoken automatically, her brain apparently stuck somewhere between asleep and awake, without regard to whom she was addressing or how he might respond.

Of course, his response was predictably male—his gaze dropped to her chest and his lips curved in a slow and sexy smile. "Yeah—I'm aware of that."

Her cheeks burned as her traitorous nipples tightened beneath the thin cotton of her ribbed tank top in response to his perusal, practically begging for his attention. She lifted her arms to reach for the baby, and to cover up her breasts. "I only meant that he prefers a softer chest to snuggle against."

"Can't blame him for that," Ryan agreed, transferring the little boy to her.

Oliver immediately dropped his head onto her shoulder and dipped a hand down the front of her top to rest on the slope of her breast.

"The kid's got some slick moves," Ryan noted.

Harper felt her cheeks burning again as she moved over to the chair and settled in to rock the baby.

"It's a comfort thing," she said, not wanting to go into any more detail than that. She knew that it had started when Melissa was trying to wean him and Oliver stubbornly refused to drink from a cup. Her doctor had suggested that he was rejecting the cup because he wanted the skin-on-skin contact of nursing. So Melissa cuddled with him as if she was nursing but gave him milk from a cup.

After a few weeks, he would happily drink from the cup so long as his hand was on her skin—and yes, she confided, that usually meant her breast. But over time, even that had become unnecessary. Losing his mother had obviously rekindled that need for skin-on-skin contact, and Harper had no intention of refusing Oliver the little comfort she could give him.

"Maybe I need to be comforted, too," Ryan teased.

She rolled her eyes. "Then maybe you should call Brittney."

He looked at her blankly. "Who?"

"The woman you were with the night I called to tell you about Melissa and Darren's accident," she prompted.

The confusion in his eyes cleared. "That was Bethany."

"I'm going to have to write down the names of all of your girlfriends in order to keep them straight."

"That won't be necessary," he said. "Because there's no reason for you to cross paths with any of them."

"Fair enough," she agreed. "So long as you're back from whatever bed you tangle the sheets in by five thirty so that I can go to work, I don't care where you sleep."

"That's what time you leave every morning? Five thirty *a.m.*?"

She nodded.

Because Oliver had been waking so frequently in the night, Ryan usually slept like the dead after he got the baby settled back down and returned to his own bed. So while he knew Harper's day started early, he hadn't realized it was quite so early. "That's insane."

"Look on the plus side," she suggested. "It will save you those awkward morning-after goodbyes."

She'd made it clear from their first meeting that she didn't hold the highest opinion of him. Even at twenty-one, not yet graduated from NYU, Harper Ross had been a woman with plans and ambitions. Ryan had been finishing up his business degree at Columbia and preparing for an entry-level position at Garrett Furniture. And although there had been some definite chemistry between them, she'd made it clear that she wanted more than a man content to work in sales.

Even when she'd found out that his family owned the multimillion-dollar company, she hadn't been impressed. In fact, she'd accused him of coasting through life on his family name and money. There was probably some truth to that, but Ryan had grown up with a workaholic father who missed more family dinners than he attended. As a result, he'd vowed not to live his life the same way and he refused to apologize for the fact.

He also refused to let her put him on the defensive about his personal relationships.

"The only awkward morning-after I ever experienced was with you," he told her.

Harper drew in a sharp breath and glared at him over the baby's head. "We agreed to *never* talk about that night."

"I didn't agree to any such thing," he denied. "You decreed it and I chose to go along."

She glanced down at Oliver, who, despite their heated exchange, had immediately settled back to sleep. "So why are you bringing it up now?" she challenged.

It was a good question—and one he wasn't sure he knew how to answer. Because even if he hadn't explicitly agreed that the subject was off-limits, he *had* gone along with her request that they both forget it had ever happened.

Except that he'd never really forgotten about that night. Yes, he wanted to—because it was more than a little humbling to share an incredible sexual experience with a woman who made it clear that it was never going to happen again—but his efforts had been unsuccessful.

No, he hadn't forgotten about that night, but he'd pretended that he could. And he'd never said a word about it to anyone. Until now.

"Because it's there," he finally said in response to her question. "Even if we don't talk about it—it's there."

"It was one night more than four years ago," she reminded him. "Ancient history."

"If it was so long ago and so unimportant, why didn't you ever tell Melissa about it?" he challenged.

"What?"

"You always said that there were no secrets between

best friends, that you told her everything. So why did you never tell her about that night?"

"Because I didn't want things to be awkward between us."

"Us *who*? You and her? You and me?"

"All of us." She kept her focus on the baby. "If I'd told Melissa, she would have told Darren. Then anytime we were all together, it would have been awkward and weird."

"You don't think it was awkward and weird anyway?"

"Not at all," she denied.

"You don't feel *any* residual attraction when we're together?"

"Hardly."

His gaze narrowed at the dismissive tone, but he noticed that she didn't look at him as she spoke. Her gaze had dropped to his shoulders, skimmed down his torso. Even in the dim light, he could tell that she was checking him out—and appreciating what she saw. "You're a smart woman, Harper."

She dragged her eyes from his bare chest to meet his again. "Thank you," she said, just a little warily.

"So you must realize that a lot of guys would take that statement as a challenge."

"It was merely a statement of fact."

He told her what he thought of that in a single-word reply.

She rose from the chair with the sleeping baby. "I'm putting Oliver in his bed and going back to my own."

He couldn't resist baiting her, just a little. "Is that an invitation?"

"Has hell frozen over?"

She responded without missing a beat, and he found himself smiling as he watched her gently lay Oliver down on his mattress. What was it about this woman that, even while she infuriated him, he couldn't help but admire her quick mind and spunky attitude?

He walked beside her to the door. "You still want me."

"You really need to do something about that ego be-fore—"

He touched a finger to her lips, silencing her words.

"You still want me," he said again. "As much as I still want you."

As he spoke, his fingertip traced the outline of her lips. Even after four years, he remembered the softness of her mouth, the sweetness of her kiss. He remembered the passion of her response to his touch and the feel of her hands moving over his body.

Her eyes darkened and the rapid flutter of the pulse point below her ear made him think that she was remembering those same things.

Then she blinked and took a deliberate step back. "Are you really hitting on me less than three weeks after we buried our best friends?"

"I was merely stating a fact," he said.

"Your slanted interpretation of a fact," she countered.

He slung an arm across the doorway, halting her retreat. "I hardly think you're in any position to be talking to me about slanted interpretations when you're deep in denial about your own feelings."

She rolled her eyes. "Because I must be in denial if I'm not dragging you across the hall to my bed, right?"

"You wouldn't have to drag me—I'd probably cooperate if you asked nicely."

"Don't hold your breath."

Chapter Two

"...available dates for next month."

The words nudged at Harper's mind as if from a distance.

She recognized her assistant's voice, but she wasn't sure Diya was talking to her and she couldn't summon the energy to respond.

"Did you hear me?"

The voice was closer now, sharper.

"Harper?"

She lifted her head, blinked her gritty eyes. "Yes, of course."

Diya's expression was concerned. "Are you okay?"

"I'm fine." She reached for the mug of coffee at her elbow and swallowed a mouthful, trying not to wince as the cold liquid slid down her throat. Obviously she'd zoned out for more than a couple of minutes if the coffee she thought she'd just poured was already cold.

She blamed Ryan for her lack of sleep the night before. After she'd put Oliver down in his bed and gone back to her own, she'd lain awake for a long time thinking about what he'd said—and silently damning him for being right.

Because she did still want him. Just being near the man made her blood heat and her heart pound. And there had been a brief moment in the doorway of Oliver's bedroom, as Ryan had slowly and gently traced the outline of her mouth with the tip of his finger, when she'd wished he would stop teasing her and start kissing her. She'd wanted to lift her hands to touch him, sliding her palms over the rippling muscles of his belly, the hard planes of his chest. And yes, dammit, she *had* wanted to drag him across the hall and have her way with him.

Of course, he probably had the same effect on most females. Because how could any woman resist the intense focus of those green-and-gold eyes that made her feel as if he saw nothing but her? How could she deny the allure of that sexy half smile that promised all kinds of sensual pleasure? Harper didn't think it was possible.

She knew that guys like that, who had women falling at their feet, were often selfish lovers—concerned only with their own satisfaction. She also knew that Ryan Garrett was *not* one of those guys.

However, one spectacular lovemaking experience more than four years earlier couldn't change the fundamental fact that they were completely and totally wrong for one another. Like her favorite Godiva salted-caramel chocolate bars—he might be tempting and delicious, but she knew she would inevitably regret the indulgence. It was that knowledge that had finally given her the strength to move away from him.

Unfortunately, the memories of that long-ago experience churned up by his casual touch had kept her awake into the early hours of morning. And wasn't it a sad reflection on her love life that, four years later, she could still recall every detail of that night?

She shook her head, as if to banish the unwelcome memories, and realized that while she'd been gathering her scattered thoughts, her assistant had taken her cold coffee cup away and returned now with a fresh, steaming cup.

"Thanks," Harper said gratefully.

"You have—" Diya gestured to her own cheek "—paper creases on your face."

So much for maintaining the illusion that she had been hard at work rather than sleeping at her desk. "I guess I dozed off for a minute," she acknowledged.

"Why don't you go home and get some proper sleep?" her assistant suggested gently.

"Because when I get home, I'm on baby duty," she admitted.

"Babies nap—you have to learn to sleep when they do."

It was the same advice she'd read in countless books, but it seemed to Harper that whenever Oliver was napping, there were a million other things to do before she could even consider sleep.

"That sounds simple enough," she agreed. "But when I put my head down on a pillow, my mind refuses to shut off."

"But when you put your head down on a desk, sleep comes?"

Her smile was wry. "Apparently."

Diya shook her head. "What are you working on there?"

She had to look at the computer screen to remember. "Finalizing the shopping list for our cooking segment tomorrow morning."

"'In the Kitchen with Kane.'" Her assistant sighed dreamily. "That man is as yummy as everything he cooks."

"And an absolute tyrant when it comes to his supplies and ingredients. Three of the items he wants for tomorrow— banana blossom, *rau ram* and Thai basil—are only available from that specialty cooking shop in Raleigh."

"What's *rau ram*?"

"Vietnamese coriander—which is apparently similar to cilantro, but Kane can't use cilantro. He *has* to have *rau ram*."

"Send the list to my phone—I'll go."

"Really?"

"Sure. My sister, Esha, lives in Raleigh and I was planning to stop by to see her this week anyway."

"That would be a huge help," Harper told her.

"I'm the assistant producer's assistant—it's my job to help," Diya reminded her.

"Well, thank you for saving me a detour to the grocery store on my way home."

"Anytime."

But as Harper was making her way to her car, her phone chimed with a text message.

can u pick up milk for Oliver?

And she realized she was going to have to make that detour anyway.

Only a few weeks earlier, Ryan had texted his brother to tell Justin that he would pick up the beer on his way over to watch the game. Today he'd texted the woman he was living with to ask her to pick up milk for the baby.

Obviously his life had undergone some major changes, not the least of which was that he was now playing house with Harper Ross. Beautiful, smart, sexy and infinitely challenging Harper Ross.

He used to think he was smart, too, but his unrelenting attraction to his co-guardian suggested otherwise. He'd been attracted to other women—a lot of other women, and he'd taken a fair number of those other women to his bed. Whether a relationship lasted a few nights or several months, it would inevitably run its course. And when it did, he and the woman in question would part ways, usually amicably.

The problem, from his perspective, was that his relationship with Harper had never run its course. One night with her hadn't been enough. Not even close. But after that first night, she'd made it clear there wouldn't be a second.

And he'd accepted her decision. He hadn't tried to change her mind. If she didn't want him, there were plenty of other women who did. Unfortunately, countless nights with other women hadn't helped him purge his desire for her. It was still Harper he wanted, her taste that he craved, her passion that he coveted. He'd hoped the yearning would fade with time and distance. Of course, their current circumstances ensured that he would have the benefit of neither of those to help assuage the ache inside him.

He heard a thump through the monitor on the counter and, glancing at the screen, saw that Oliver had kicked the headboard of his crib. The kid was a restless sleeper. He always started in the middle of the mattress, but he never finished there. He sometimes woke up on his belly, sometimes on his back, but never in the same position he'd started from. Ryan figured it was a good thing Oliver's bed had four sides—otherwise the little guy might wake up in the hall.

As he dumped some pasta into a pot, he kept an ear tuned to the monitor, listening for any other indications that Oliver was waking up from his nap. For now, he was sleeping peacefully, blissfully unaware that the "mama" and "dada" he still called out for weren't ever coming home again. Ryan tried not to dwell on that fact too much himself, but it was an unassailable truth that squeezed like a fist around his heart.

He missed his friend. He hated that Darren's life had ended so tragically and prematurely only weeks after his thirtieth birthday. And there were moments, though he would never acknowledge them aloud, when he resented having his own life derailed by the responsibility of helping to raise Darren and Melissa's child.

Those moments never lasted long—probably not more than a few seconds. Just long enough for the thought to form and guilt to slice him in half. Because how could he be mad at his friend for anything when Darren had lost everything? How could he begrudge caring for his best friend's son when the little boy already owned his heart?

Maybe Ryan had never given much thought to being a father, but he knew that Darren had been as excited as Melissa when they'd learned she was expecting their first child. And even when Ryan had teased his friend about trading in his Audi for a minivan, Darren hadn't minded. He'd been sincerely looking forward to Cub Scouts and soccer games and all the things that most dads did with their sons.

But he hadn't had a chance to do any of them, so Ryan would. He'd even buy that minivan if he had to—but he really hoped he wouldn't have to. A Jeep, maybe. Yeah, a Jeep had enough seats for carpooling and plenty of cargo space for all of the kids' gear.

The timer on the oven buzzed. He lifted the pot off the stove and dumped the macaroni into a colander just as Harper came through the back door with the jug of milk he needed to make the cheese sauce.

Her heels clicked on the ceramic tile, drawing his attention to the sexy sling-back shoes on her feet. His gaze skimmed upward, following the curve of her calves to the flirty hem of her skirt, which twirled around her knees—

"Is Oliver still sleeping?"

He dragged his attention away from her legs. "Yeah, but he's moving around in his crib, so probably not for long." He dumped the pasta back into the pot and reached for the milk, frowned at the label. "This is nonfat milk."

"So?" She kicked off her shoes and dropped her purse on the counter.

"So Oliver can't drink that."

"Why not?"

"Because babies need whole milk until the age of two, to aid in brain development."

She huffed out an impatient breath. "Your message didn't say to pick up whole milk—it just said milk."

"I figured you knew."

"Well, obviously you figured wrong," she snapped at him, as she slipped her feet back into her shoes and grabbed her purse again.

"Where are you going?"

"To get whole milk."

Clearly, he'd screwed up. Again. Eager to smooth things over, he told her, "Don't worry. This'll be fine for his pasta. I'll go out later and—"

"You asked me to get it," she reminded him, reaching for the handle of the door.

He slapped his hand on the frame so that she couldn't open it. "Forget it. It's not that big of a deal."

But he could tell by the moisture shimmering in her eyes that it was—at least to her.

He wondered how it was that, only ten minutes earlier, he'd been thinking that they were managing okay and now

Harper was on the verge of a meltdown—for reasons he couldn't even begin to fathom.

"Haven't you ever heard the saying 'no use crying over spilled milk'?" he asked, striving for lightness in a desperate attempt to ward off her tears. "Well, I think the same could be said about nonfat milk."

"I'm not crying," she denied.

And maybe she wasn't, but she definitely sniffled.

"Do you want to tell me what this is really about?" he asked gently.

She shook her head. "I'm just tired."

Which was hardly surprising in light of the hours that she worked—not just at the studio but after Oliver was settled into bed at night. "It's almost the weekend—you can sleep all day Saturday if you want."

"I don't mean physically tired, although I am that, too," she admitted. "I mean tired of faking it."

His brows lifted. "What exactly have you been faking?"

She drew in a deep breath and looked up at him. "That I know what I'm doing here, playing house, playing *mommy*, when the truth is, I don't have a clue."

He tucked a strand of hair behind her ear, then cupped the back of her head and gently drew her closer, until her forehead was against his shoulder. "You're doing just fine. *We're* doing just fine."

She didn't pull back, but she shook her head again. "You already do so much more than I do, and when you ask me to do one little thing, I screw it up."

"No one's keeping score, Harper."

"If they were, you'd get all the points," she said.

"That's not true," he denied. "You'd get points for having breasts."

That, finally, earned him a watery smile.

"Now, why don't you go get Oliver while I finish making the mac and cheese?" he suggested. "There's enough for you, too, if you're hungry."

"Maybe." And then, proving she hadn't lost her sense of humor, she added, "But only if you're making it with nonfat milk."

She didn't have any of the pasta.

Instead Harper made herself a salad and munched on lettuce and chopped veggies while Oliver shoved handfuls of macaroni in his mouth and smeared cheese sauce all over his face and the tray of his high chair.

Ryan had taken his bowl of pasta into the main-floor den to do some work while awaiting the start of a conference call. In the past, Harper might have resented the inherent flexibility afforded to him because his family owned the business he worked for. Now she was grateful.

Not just because it allowed them to share childcare responsibilities but because their offsetting schedules meant that they didn't have to spend a lot of time together. Because their late-night encounter the night before had reminded her all too clearly how dangerous it was to be in close proximity to Ryan Garrett.

"Mo!" Oliver demanded, banging his now-empty bowl on his tray.

"Please," Harper admonished.

"Mo!" he said again.

She got up to put some more macaroni in his bowl, shook her head when she placed it in front of him. "You are a mess."

"Mess," he echoed, and grinned to show off his eight tiny pearly-white teeth in a mouth stuffed full of macaroni.

Smiling, she ruffled the soft, wispy curls that fell over his forehead.

He needed a haircut—his first haircut. A few months

earlier, Melissa had told her that Darren was pushing her to take Oliver to the barbershop because he was tired of strangers mistakenly assuming their son was a daughter, even when he was dressed all in blue. Melissa had resisted, because she was afraid that if they cut off Oliver's curls, they might be gone forever. And just in case, she'd already snipped one of them and tucked it into a clear plastic folder in his baby book.

The baby book that Melissa kept in the top drawer of Oliver's dresser so it was readily accessible to record her son's every milestone. She'd documented everything from his weight and length at birth and the day he came home from the hospital to his first smile, when he rolled over, sat up, clapped his hands, waved bye-bye, got his first tooth and took his first step.

It was a meticulous record of her love as much as her baby's growth, and Harper didn't know if she should continue what Melissa had started or leave the book as she had left it. Either way, she knew she had to talk to Ryan about taking the little boy for a haircut.

Sooner rather than later if he was going to insist on putting things like cheesy macaroni in it.

"I think that's a sign that you've had enough to eat," she said to him.

"Mo!"

She shook her head. "No more. Not today."

"Kee."

She was starting to understand his unique baby language and that word was one of his favorites. "Let's get you cleaned up first. Then you can have a cookie."

She wiped his hands and his face—and his hair—with a wet cloth, ensuring that no traces of orange sauce remained. "There's my handsome boy," she said.

He grinned at her, melting her heart. "Kee."

She laughed. "Yes, I'll get you a cookie."

While he was munching on his arrowroot biscuit, she tidied up the kitchen. Then she washed Oliver's hands and face again.

"What are we going to do this afternoon?" she asked the little boy.

He banged his hands on his tray. "Bah-bah-bah."

"I'm going to need a translation on that," she said as she unbuckled him from his high chair. "Either you want to play ball or you want to pretend you're a sheep—which is it?"

"Bah-bah-bah."

"Blocks," Ryan said from the doorway.

Harper glanced up as she set the little boy on his feet. He ran straight to Ryan, who swung him up into his arms. "Do you want to play with your blocks?"

"Bah-bah-bah."

Harper frowned as she moved into the living room. "Do you think his speech is delayed?"

"No, I think he's a sixteen-month-old with the limited vocabulary of a sixteen-month-old."

He was probably right but she thought she'd check the vocabulary lists in her books again to be sure. "Your conference call is done already?"

He nodded. "I knew it wouldn't take too long."

She put the bucket of blocks on the carpet and sat down to play with Oliver. The little boy immediately upended the container. "Are you going into the office now?"

"Not today."

She started the base of a tower for Oliver, aligning three square blocks for the bottom, then overlapping a second row to hold the blocks together. "Why not?"

"I thought I'd spend some time hanging out with Oliver this afternoon."

"Big," Oliver said again, offering her a blue block.

"He wants you to make the tower bigger," Ryan told her, squatting down to add more blocks to the base of the structure she'd started to build.

"You just want to play, too," she remarked.

He didn't dispute her claim. "Do you have a problem with that?"

"You had Oliver all morning—it's my shift now," she reminded him.

"Just like no one's keeping score, no one's punching a clock here," he said gently. "If there's something else you'd rather be doing, I don't mind honing my construction skills here."

She hesitated, torn between the temptation to accept his offer, annoyance that he handled the little boy so effortlessly and guilt that if she let him, she would again be doing less than her share. "I do have some notes to write up for Caroline for next week's shows."

He shrugged. "Or you could take a nap so you're not cranky tomorrow."

"I'm not cranky now," she snapped, her tone in contradiction to the words.

He just lifted a brow.

She turned on her heel and walked out.

Chapter Three

Harper hadn't planned to fall asleep.

She'd decided that her notes for Caroline could wait, and she'd lain down on her bed to read another chapter in *What to Expect the Toddler Years*. She managed to keep her eyes open for four pages.

When she woke up, it was almost five o'clock and her grumbling stomach chastised her for not thinking about dinner before she'd put her head on her pillow. After a quick detour to the bathroom, she headed down to the kitchen to see what she could scrounge up for the evening meal.

But Ryan had apparently beat her to that, too, as he was peeling potatoes at the sink. Oliver was on the floor nearby, playing with some plastic lids. They both glanced over when she stepped through the doorway.

"I guess I should say 'sorry' and 'thank you.'"

"Why?"

"The 'sorry' because I was tired and cranky. The 'thank you' for letting me sleep and getting dinner started."

"No worries," he said easily.

"What's for supper?"

"Steak pie, mashed potatoes and corn."

"Do you want me to finish the potatoes?"

"Are you going to eat any potatoes?"

"Probably not," she admitted.

"Then you can make your salad."

She got the ingredients out of the fridge and set to work.

Half an hour later, they were sitting down to dinner, just like a regular family.

Except that she had almost no experience being a regular family. She'd grown up in New York City, where her father was an actor and her mother was a talent agent. And for as long as Harper could remember, her parents had been going in opposite directions—to auditions and meetings and events. Occasionally one or the other would take her and her brother, Spencer, along for the ride, but more often they were left at home with the nanny.

The unconventional upbringing was something she'd had in common with Melissa. Her friend's parents had split when she was in the third grade, and after that she'd done her share of moving from one home to another, never feeling as if she completely belonged in either. As a result, she'd been determined to provide a better upbringing for her son—and a "normal" home in which parents sat down to share meals with their children. Harper wasn't convinced that was "normal" but she was willing to do her part to maintain at least the illusion for the little boy.

"This pie is delicious," she said after she'd sampled her first bite.

Obviously Oliver agreed, because he was managing

to put more of the steak and gravy in his mouth than on his face.

"One of my aunt Susan's specialties," Ryan told her. "I can only take credit for moving it from the freezer to the oven."

"Between your mother and your aunts and your cousins, we probably have enough pies and casseroles and pastas to last until Christmas."

"My family has always believed that food can help alleviate any crisis."

"That much food would solve the hunger crisis in a third-world country."

"My mother also knows that I can burn toast," Ryan said. "And she probably didn't want to make any assumptions about your cooking skills."

"I can put together a decent meal if I have the time and the right ingredients," she admitted.

"I wasn't sure," he teased. "Because I haven't seen you eat anything other than salad."

"That's not true," she denied.

"You're right—salad and a taste of whatever else is put on the table."

Since that was closer to the truth, she didn't dispute it. Instead she said, "Even over and above the stocking of our freezer, your family has been amazing. Although there were so many people here the day of the funeral, I'm not sure I remember even half of their names."

"I'll make name tags for the next family gathering," he teased.

"That would be helpful," she said, her response perfectly sincere. "But for starters, which one of your bothers has the little boy—Jacob?"

"Jacob is Daniel's son—but Daniel is my cousin. Braden and Justin are my brothers."

"Justin is the doctor?"

He nodded.

"Is he married?"

"No."

"But Braden's married?"

He nodded again. "To Dana."

"Do they have any kids?"

"Not yet."

"And you have a sister who has a baby girl, right?"

"Nope—no sisters at all. You're probably thinking of Lauryn, who is another cousin."

She frowned. "But she referred to you as her daughter's 'uncle Ryan.'"

"It's an honorary title."

Harper shook her head. "No wonder I'm confused."

"Andrew, Nathan and Daniel are my cousins through my uncle David and aunt Jane. Andrew is married to Rachel and the father of Maura. Nathan is married to Allison, who is the mother of Dylan. And Jacob's father, Daniel, is married to Kenna.

"On my uncle Thomas and aunt Susan's side, there are three female cousins—Jordyn, Tristyn and Lauryn. Lauryn is the only one married, and she and her husband, Rob, are the parents of Kylie.

"I also have three more cousins—Matthew, Jackson and Lukas—in upstate New York. Matt and his wife, Georgia, have four kids, Jack and Kelly have two, and Lukas and Julie have a toddler."

"Name tags would definitely help," she told him.

He just grinned. "What about your family?"

"Small," she said. "And scattered. My dad has a sister who works for an insurance company in Wyoming, but she never married and doesn't have any kids. His mother is down in Florida, but I haven't seen her since I was a kid.

My mom was an only child, so there's just my parents, myself and my brother."

None of whom had shown up for the funeral, despite the fact that Melissa had been her roommate in college and her best friend since.

Gayle Everton-Ross had expressed sympathy when her daughter called to tell her about the tragic heli-skiing accident that killed Melissa and Darren, but she hadn't been able to talk long, because she was on her way to a meeting. Peter Ross had been busy on the set of the popular soap opera *The Light of Dawn*, and Spencer, an underwear model and wannabe actor, had been playing a bit part in an Off-Off-Broadway production.

"Are you close?" Ryan asked.

She shook her head. "Melissa was more my family than anyone I'm actually related to."

"I have brothers and cousins," he said again, "but Darren was my family, too."

"I know."

They finished their meals in silence. Even Oliver was quiet while he ate, more interested in his food than any attempt at communication. As Harper picked at her salad, she found her thoughts wandering. She'd met Ryan, through Melissa and Darren, more than six years earlier, but she wouldn't have said that she knew him well. And while they were friendly enough, they weren't friends—they were too different for that.

They'd occasionally hung out together, usually in a group, but they didn't have much in common and never really hit it off. Even when Melissa and Darren got engaged and asked Harper and Ryan to be their maid of honor and best man respectively, they didn't work particularly well together. She'd claimed he was too laid-back and he'd accused her of being too uptight, but they'd managed to put their personal differences aside for the benefit of their friends.

Then came the wedding night—when Harper ended up in Ryan's bed. The next morning, they both agreed it was a mistake, and neither of them ever told anyone else what had happened.

When Oliver was born, the proud parents again turned to their best friends, asking them to be godparents and co-guardians of their baby. They'd both agreed, neither of them willing to let a little bit of personal history get in the way of their friends' wishes. Of course, neither of them had anticipated that the guardianship would ever mean anything more than their names on a piece of paper.

Now, only a few months later, they had to figure out a way to work together for the sake of the little boy. Because the reality was that there wasn't anyone else who could take care of Oliver.

She was certain of that because she'd spent a fair amount of time over the past few weeks trying to figure out if there were any other options—and desperately hoping, for Oliver's sake, that there were.

Celeste Trivitt, his maternal grandmother, lived in France with her investment banker husband. She'd been devastated to hear of the accident that took her daughter's life and immediately flew in for the funeral. Although she was happy to fuss over her grandson for a few days, she'd made it clear that her life was in Europe now. Oliver was lucky, she'd said to them more than once. He might have lost both of his parents, but he had Harper and Ryan to take care of him.

Quentin Trivitt, Oliver's maternal grandfather and Celeste's ex-husband, also came for the funeral—with his thirty-four-year-old wife, who was seven months pregnant with their first child. They'd said all the right things, expressing empathy for the "poor little boy" and his situation but at the same time making it clear that their focus was on their own yet-to-be-born child. They had no interest in raising a grandson, too.

On the other side, Oliver's paternal grandparents were both living in an assisted-care facility in Greensboro. One of the attendants from the home had brought them to Charisma for the funeral and taken them right back again. Darren also had a sister, but neither Ryan nor Harper had ever met her and no one had known how to reach her to tell her about the passing of her brother and sister-in-law. Harper remembered Melissa telling her that Darren's sister had been estranged from her family for a long time.

Harper pushed away from the table and carried her plate, with half of her meal still on it, to the counter. "Do you ever wonder…?"

Ryan began clearing the rest of the dishes. "What?"

She hesitated to say the words out loud, as if doing so might be disloyal to her friend, but she finally said, "If maybe Melissa and Darren should have chosen someone else to take care of Oliver?"

"Every day," he told her.

"Really?"

He nodded. "But I figure they must have had their reasons for choosing us."

"Maybe," she allowed. "I'm just not sure I'm the right person to do this."

"I have more than a few doubts about my suitability, too," he said, surprising her with the acknowledgment. "But I'm not going to walk away without giving it my best shot."

She squirted dish soap in the sink and turned on the faucet. "You think I want to walk away?"

"I don't know—do you?"

She considered the question as she watched the sudsy

water rise in the bowl. "Yes," she finally admitted. "There is part of me that wants to do exactly that."

"And another part?" he prompted.

Harper plunged her hands into the water and began to wash the pots. "We had a long talk when Melissa asked if I would be the baby's guardian," she said, not directly answering his question. "While she was pregnant, when he was still 'the baby' and not yet Oliver. I thought it was strange that she would be thinking about such things before her child was even born, but Melissa always did like to be prepared, to run her life according to a specific plan."

"It's a good thing she did," Ryan said. "Because Darren wouldn't know a plan if it bit him in the butt."

She smiled at that. "True. Anyway, I asked her—why me? Aside from the fact that I was her best friend, what made her think I could ever be the right choice to help raise her child?"

Harper remembered every word of their conversation, could still hear the echo of her friend's voice in the back of her mind so clearly that it made her chest ache and her throat burn.

"What did she say?" Ryan prompted gently.

"That she chose me because she knew if anything ever happened to her so that she couldn't raise her child, I would love him as much as she did," she confided. "And that's the part that won't let me walk away—the echo of Melissa's voice in my mind, asking me to love her little boy for her. Because I already do."

He touched a hand to her shoulder. "Then I'd say it's obvious that she made the right choice."

Harper still wasn't convinced, but she knew that she wasn't going to let down her friend. Not if she could help it.

* * *

Ryan considered it progress that he and Harper had actually managed to have a fifteen-minute conversation without sniping at one another. It was a minor step, and he knew they were going to have to do a lot better than that if they were going to figure out a way to make this guardianship situation work for Oliver, but at least it was a step in the right direction.

Considering that he'd known her for so many years, he really didn't know her at all. And maybe that was his fault. He'd never made much of an effort, because it had seemed like too much of an effort.

The first time he'd met her, he'd been willing to consider all kinds of possibilities. Darren had assured him that it wasn't a setup; it was just his girlfriend wanting his best friend to meet her best friend. And since Ryan liked Melissa well enough, he'd figured he'd like her friend, too.

And he had. Harper was attractive—even more so than he'd hoped. About five-five, he'd guessed, with brown hair and dark chocolate-colored eyes. She was a little on the skinny side, but her perfectly shaped lips enticed him to hang on to her every word.

They'd talked about college: she was studying journalism at NYU and hoped to work in television; he was in his final year of business at Columbia. She'd asked about his future plans, he'd said that he didn't have any specific plans, and she'd shut down.

It wasn't exactly the truth—he'd always known that he would go to work at Garrett Furniture, but he'd learned to be cautious about revealing his connection to the company. Too many women wanted to be with him because he was a Garrett and heir to at least part of the furniture empire of the same name.

Harper had decided then and there that he lacked ambition. Later, when she found out that he was one of *the* Garretts, the information had done nothing to bolster her opinion of him. In fact, she'd insisted that it only proved he was too lazy to make his own way outside the family business. He didn't care what she thought—he liked what he did and enjoyed being part of the continued success of the company his grandfather had built.

Yet despite the obvious personality conflicts between Harper and himself, there was an undeniable sizzle in the air whenever they were together. It had been there from the start and was still there. Even when one or the other—or both—had been dating someone else, the air fairly vibrated with electricity between them. It was a phenomenon that he found as baffling as it was intriguing.

Not that he'd had any intention of ever acting upon it. Especially considering that Harper had always given a clear and unequivocal hands-off vibe…right up until the night that she'd begged him to put his hands *on* her.

And that was definitely *not* something that he should be thinking about now.

Going forward, he had to keep his focus on Oliver and not let himself be distracted by the memory of Harper's warm, naked body wrapped around his.

"You are doing a great job with Oliver," he said now, as he helped load the dishwasher. "But between your work schedule and the demands of a grieving infant, it's obvious that you're exhausted."

"I'm so flattered that you noticed."

His brow lifted in response to her sarcasm. "I'm dragging, too, and I'm only working part-time right now."

"Part-time isn't an option for me."

"Then maybe you should think about taking some time off."

"I did think about it," she said bluntly. "I can't."

He pressed on anyway. "You went back to work only days after the funeral—when did you think about it?"

"In the time between learning about the accident and returning to work," she told him. "I would have taken more time if I could, but there's too much going on with the show right now. In fact, we've got Lucy Gibbs on the schedule for tomorrow morning, so I have to go in half an hour earlier because she likes to review all of the questions with me beforehand."

"She can't do that with someone else?"

"The last time she was on the show and I wasn't there, she bullied and harassed one of our production assistants to the point that he almost quit."

"She sounds charming," he said drily.

She shrugged. "It doesn't matter that she's a prima donna when her name is money at the box office."

"If you're going in early, will you be able to leave early?"

"I'm going to try," she said. "But there were a couple of day-care centers that I wanted to check out on my way back."

He frowned. "You want to put Oliver in day care?"

"I don't see that we have any choice." She neatly folded the dishcloth and draped it over the towel bar inside the cupboard.

"Don't you think we should talk about this—to see if we can't figure something else out? For God's sake, Harper, the kid just lost both of his parents and you want to abdicate responsibility for his care to strangers?"

"It's not what I want. It's what the reality of the situation demands." She braced her hands on the edge of the counter behind her and faced him. "I don't have the luxury of working for a company owned by my family," she told him. "If I don't go to work, I don't get paid."

"If the issue is money, I'll pay—"

"No." She cut him off sharply. "It's not only about money."

"I know how important your career is to you," he said.

But Harper didn't think he did. Because her career was more than important—it was what defined her.

She'd started as an assistant to the property manager at WNCC-TV fresh out of college and worked her way through the ranks to become an associate producer of the award-winning morning program *Coffee Time with Caroline*. In the process, she'd sacrificed weekends and vacations, missed get-togethers with friends, turned down more offers for dates than she'd accepted—and then skipped out early on at least half of those that she'd accepted.

Ryan, on the other hand, had been born a Garrett. He'd never had to make any sacrifices to secure his job at Garrett Furniture. Maybe he hadn't started out as national sales manager of the company, but there hadn't been a lot of obstacles in his path to the big office.

He didn't have to worry that taking a few weeks off might jeopardize his position, but Harper knew that a leave of absence—even in the short term—could completely derail her career.

"I just don't think we should rush into anything," he continued, his tone conciliatory.

But she'd learned the hard way that if she didn't take action, things didn't get done. "How much longer should we wait? Another couple of weeks? A month?"

"More than three weeks," he retorted.

She forced herself to take a deep breath before their discussion escalated into a full-blown argument. "I did some research and made some phone calls. I'm not suggesting we drop him off somewhere first thing tomorrow morning."

He nodded slowly as he wiped Oliver's hands and face. "What day cares are you considering?"

That he asked suggested that he might come around on the issue, and because she needed his cooperation to make it work, she answered in an equally careful tone. "First Steps and Wee Watch are the only ones that are on the short list so far. Little Hands looked good, too, but its location isn't convenient for either of us."

"Andrew's daughter, Maura, went to Wee Watch."

"So that would be your choice?"

"My choice would be to figure out a way to coordinate our schedules so that Oliver doesn't have to go to day care."

She folded her arms over her chest. "Well, I work every day from six a.m. until noon, sometimes with production meetings afterward. Can you work your schedule around that?"

"Do you understand the word *compromise*?"

"Yes, I do. But I'm not willing to compromise my job."

"I'm not asking you to. I'm only asking you to pause to take a breath, to give all of us—and especially Oliver—some time to come to terms with everything that's happened."

"That sounds great in theory, but the last three weeks have been complete chaos and I need to get things settled and get my life back on track."

"Do you really think anyone at work needs you more than this little boy—" he picked Oliver up out of his high chair "—does right now?"

"No—but at least at the studio, I know what I'm doing."

It wasn't something she'd planned to admit, especially not to Ryan. But the truth was, even after only three weeks, it was apparent that he was much more comfortable with Oliver and much better at anticipating the little boy's needs than she was, making her feel not just inept but dependent on him.

And that was why she needed to focus on her work: because it was the only place right now that she felt competent and in control. When she was with Oliver and Ryan, she felt overwhelmed and helpless and all kinds of other emotions she wasn't ready to acknowledge, much less put a label on.

Chapter Four

Ryan wasn't usually awake at 5:00 a.m.—and he didn't understand why any sane person would be. But Thursday night, Oliver was even more restless than usual, waking at midnight, then 2:00 a.m. and again at 3:00 and 4:00.

As a result, Ryan fell asleep in the rocking chair with the little guy in his arms and heard Harper's alarm go off forty-five minutes later. Then he heard the shower start, and there was no going back to sleep for him after that. Because thinking about Harper in the shower teased him with mental images of her sexy body naked and wet, and suddenly certain parts of him were very wide-awake.

Not wide-awake enough to want to get dressed and go into work, as Harper did at that ungodly hour five days a week. He didn't know anything about television, but it seemed crazy to him that she had to be at the studio at six o'clock in the morning for a show that didn't go on the air until ten. Even more surprising was the fact that she genuinely seemed to enjoy her job.

Coffee Time with Caroline was an hour-long program, but Harper didn't leave the studio when filming was done. Instead she went back to her office to review any problems or concerns with the staff and prepare for the next day's program.

He didn't usually get to his office at Garrett Furniture before two o'clock, which meant that he was often in meetings or conference calls with other salespeople from then until five, when everyone else went home because their day had started at a normal hour. It was hardly an ideal situation, but so far it was working for them. Not seamlessly but satisfactorily.

Day care would simplify both of their lives—he couldn't deny that. He also agreed that Oliver could benefit from an environment shared with other children and the exposure to alternate routines. But he still believed it was too soon. There had been too many changes in the little guy's life recently to throw another one at him right now.

He'd never envisioned himself as a "Mr. Mom" kind of guy, but he found that he was enjoying his time with Oliver. They were establishing their own morning routines, which usually included sitting down in front of the television every morning at 10:00 a.m. to watch *Coffee Time with Caroline*. Though they didn't see Harper on TV, it was fun to view the end product of her work.

The first fifteen minutes of the show were spent on casual banter between Caroline and her headline guest/cohost, which was followed up by various segments with other guests. Sometimes they were celebrities on tour to promote one thing or another; other times the guests provided a more local flavor.

Every Monday, there was an SPCA spotlight to show some of the cats and dogs that were available for adoption at the local shelter; the Tuesday program included a trivia game with contestants chosen from the audience; Wednesday offered some kind of cooking segment—either the chef of a local restaurant or tips from moms for quick healthy meals; Thursday there was a "book chat"; and Friday focused on home improvement and decor.

Today's guest was Ryder Wallace—of the locally produced reality series *Ryder to the Rescue*—demonstrating the proper way to lay floor tile. Ryan thought his cousin Lauryn should get her husband, Rob, to watch the program, because God and everyone else knew that Rob couldn't even hang a picture straight. As Ryder explained the intricacies of grout application, Oliver's eyes grew heavy, and by the time the end credits rolled, the little guy was asleep.

Ryan knew that Andrew didn't like to spend more than a few hours every day in his office at Garrett Furniture, so he was grateful when he stopped by the following Monday and found his cousin was there. He poured himself a cup of coffee and settled into a chair across from the desk. "You're keeping more consistent office hours than I am these days."

"Not by choice," Andrew assured him.

Although his cousin's official title was VP of research and design, he still considered himself a carpenter and preferred working with wood to pushing paper.

"Yours or mine," Ryan agreed.

"No one objects to you taking whatever time you need to adjust to your life being turned upside down."

He nodded, grateful for the understanding. Of course, that was why he'd come to see Andrew—because he knew that he would understand. Several years earlier, his cousin had experienced something similar when Nina—his first wife—died suddenly and unexpectedly, leaving him a widower and a single father to their young daughter.

"How did you get through it?" Ryan asked him now.

"I honestly don't remember," his cousin said. "I lived in a fog for a long time after Nina's death, just going through the motions of every day—and I only managed that much for Maura."

Ryan sipped his coffee and considered the question that niggled at the back of his mind. He'd come to Andrew for information and advice, but he didn't want to appear insensitive. Although his cousin had moved on with his life and was married to Rachel now, he didn't imagine it was easy to talk about the loss of his first wife—or the impact of her death on their daughter.

But he finally ventured to ask, "Does Maura remember her mother at all?"

"I'm not sure. She was only three when Nina died. There are pictures of her in Maura's room, and we talk about her at appropriate times. And, of course, her maternal grandparents are always telling her how much she looks like her mother and reminding her how much Nina loved her."

"But she calls Rachel 'Mom' now, doesn't she?"

Andrew nodded. "That was her choice. I think because all of her friends have moms, it meant a lot for her to have someone in that role, too."

"Oliver still doesn't say very much, so what he's going to call me and Harper in the future isn't really of concern right now."

"What is?"

"Everything else," he admitted.

His cousin's smile was wry. "Welcome to fatherhood."

"I thought I had a lot more years before anyone would say those words to me." He scrubbed a hand over his jaw. "I don't know if I can do this—be a father to my best friend's little boy."

"Except that you are doing it," his cousin pointed out.

"I have these moments—a lot of moments—when I find myself floundering and wish I could call Darren. From the minute that Oliver was born, he instinctively knew what to do." He stared at the dregs of coffee in the bottom of his cup and quietly admitted, "I miss him. Every single day, I miss him. And then I think about Oliver, about how lost and confused he must feel. In one fell swoop, life as he knew it was destroyed—and somehow, I'm supposed to help him pick up the pieces."

"You don't have to do it on your own," Andrew said.

"I know, but Harper and I seem to work better together if we're not."

"I'm sure it's been a difficult adjustment for both of you—instant parenthood under a shared roof with a virtual stranger."

"Neither of us is getting much sleep because Oliver's up several times in the night."

Andrew winced. "I remember those nights—a lot of those nights. They're not fun for anyone."

"Least of all Oliver," Ryan agreed. "It breaks my heart when he wakes up asking for 'mama' or 'dada.'"

"As hard as it was for both Maura and I when we lost Nina, we at least had one another."

"Poor Oliver's stuck with me and Harper."

"I'd say Oliver's lucky to have you and Harper."

"He'd be luckier—and drier—if she knew how to change a diaper," he grumbled.

His cousin looked surprised. "She doesn't?"

"I'm actually not sure. Every time he needs to be changed, she shoves him at me."

Andrew chuckled. "Apparently she's as smart as she is beautiful."

Ryan didn't doubt that she was. Smart and beautiful and sexy and sweet, and she was frustrating the hell out of him—which was not something he intended to talk to his cousin about.

He set his empty mug aside and stood up. "Since I'm here, I should spend some time in my own office and let you sneak out of yours."

"Sounds good to me," Andrew agreed. "But if you ever need anything, anytime, let me know."

Ryan nodded. "Thanks."

He wasn't in the habit of dumping his problems on his family, but it was nice to know that they were there if he needed them. As he intended to be there for Oliver—and Harper.

Because the more time they spent together, the more he was beginning to realize that she needed them every bit as much as they needed her.

Harper had been in the habit of spending an hour at the gym after leaving the studio each day, but she hadn't been doing that since she moved into Melissa and Darren's house to take care of Oliver. While Ryan had been great about manipulating his schedule to accommodate her work hours, she didn't think it was fair to put him further behind in his own schedule for her personal workout. So for now her exercise was walking with Oliver.

Thankfully, he was content in his stroller, happy to watch the world go by as he was pushed around. She'd usually take the long way around to the park, and then she'd let the little boy play on the toddler climber and baby swings for a while before they headed home again.

Today when she unbuckled Oliver and helped him out of the stroller, he bypassed the climbing structure and raced over to the baby swings.

He grabbed hold of the plastic seat. "Whee! Whee!"

The slender blonde woman pushing another little boy

on the adjacent swing chuckled in response to Oliver's demand. "He knows what he wants, doesn't he?"

"He certainly does," Harper agreed. She smiled at the blonde as she lifted Oliver into the swing, then did a double take. "Have we met?"

The other woman nodded. "At the funeral. I'm Kenna Garrett—my husband, Daniel, is Ryan's cousin. And this—" she gave her little boy another gentle push "—is Jacob."

Harper fastened the belt around Oliver's middle. "I'm usually pretty good with names, but there were so many people there that day."

"No need to apologize," Kenna assured her. "You had a lot of more important things on your mind that day."

"Whee!" Oliver demanded.

"Whee!" Jacob echoed.

Kenna chuckled and Harper pulled back Oliver's swing and set it in motion.

"How is Oliver doing?" Kenna asked.

"The days are good," Harper said. "But he still wakes up in the middle of the night almost every night crying for his mama."

Kenna's eyes misted. "Poor fella."

Harper nodded.

"That's got to be hard on you, too. I remember how constantly exhausted I was before Jacob started sleeping through the night."

"Thankfully, because I have to get up so early, Ryan has been dealing with most of the middle-of-the-night stuff."

"That's right—he told me you work on *Coffee Time with Caroline*," Kenna recalled.

"Do you watch it?"

"Faithfully," Kenna assured her. "I started tuning in when I was on mat leave and I got hooked, so when I went back to work in the fall, I had to DVR it."

"Went back to work doing what?" Harper asked.

"I teach science at South Ridge High School."

"Sounds challenging."

"It's a piece of cake compared to being a stay-at-home mom," Kenna assured her. "And yet there are still days—most days, in fact—when I wonder if I made the right choice. But school will be out for the summer in eight weeks, and then I'll be able to devote myself to being a wife and a mother."

"Who looks after Jacob while you're working?"

"Daniel mostly works from home now, and his mother helps out *a lot*. Early on I suggested that we look into day care, and she was devastated to think that I'd prefer to have strangers looking after her grandson. Which wasn't true, of course—I was just worried that it might seem we were taking advantage of her."

"It's nice to have family support," Harper agreed.

"You've got it, too, you know," Kenna told her.

She nodded. "And I'm grateful. I honestly don't know how we would have managed without the help of Ryan's parents, especially those first few days after the accident."

"I can't imagine," Kenna said sincerely. "I had nine months to get used to the idea of having a baby. Actually, forty weeks and two days, since Jacob wasn't in any hurry to be born. And during that time, I read everything I could about childbirth and babies and what to expect and I thought I was prepared. But the reality is, no one can ever completely prepare you for the joy and responsibility of being a mother—as I'm sure you've already realized with Oliver."

"I'm not his mother," Harper felt compelled to point out—partly because she didn't want anyone to think she was trying to take Melissa's place in her son's life and partly because the title of mother terrified her even more than the responsibilities of being a caregiver.

"Maybe not biologically," Kenna acknowledged. "But in every other way that matters."

Harper knew it was true, and she felt a pang deep in her heart for the little boy who would never really know the woman who had given him life or how very much she'd loved him. She would tell him, of course. She would do everything in her power to ensure that he never forgot his mother, but she knew that he was too young to really hold on to any of the memories that he had.

"When Melissa asked me to be his godmother, I didn't hesitate. She was my best friend, and I loved Oliver from the minute he was born. But I never thought I would actually have to do anything more than take him on occasional trips to the zoo or museums and buy him fabulous presents."

"I'm sure she thought the same thing," Kenna said sympathetically.

Ryan worked late that night, and when he got home, Harper was getting Oliver's bedtime snack of oatmeal and banana ready.

They chatted a little about their respective days—he told her about the plans for Garrett Furniture's upcoming annual summer picnic and she told him about meeting Kenna and Jacob at the park. Though the conversation was easy, he detected a hint of coolness in her tone—the likely cause of which was revealed by her next comment.

"The receipt for your dry cleaning is on the counter," she told him as she settled Oliver into his high chair. "Along with the note from Nadine Deacon that was in the pocket of the jacket you wore for the funeral."

He'd forgotten about the note—probably two seconds after Nadine had slipped it into his pocket.

"Maybe I shouldn't be surprised, but I actually thought

you'd managed to refrain from hitting on women at your best friend's funeral."

Her comment chafed, as she'd no doubt intended. Maybe he did have a reputation for enjoying the company of various and beautiful women—and he wasn't going to apologize for it—but he wasn't an indiscriminate womanizer.

"I didn't ask for her number—she gave it to me and told me to call if she could help with anything."

"Oh, well, that's different, then," she said, in a tone that indicated it was not. "Although I'm not sure that Brittney would agree."

"Bethany," he reminded her.

Oliver blew a raspberry, spraying cereal and banana out of his mouth. Harper used his bib to wipe his chin, then offered him another spoonful.

"And you're hardly in a position to criticize me when you were chatting up the long-haired guy with the polished loafers."

"Simon Moore was the real estate agent who sold this house to Melissa and Darren. He came to pay his respects."

"Are you saying that he didn't give you his number?"

"He gave me his business card," she acknowledged. "In case we decided to sell."

"We're not selling their house."

She scraped the last of the oatmeal out of the bowl. "That's an emotional rather than a rational response."

"How would you know?" he challenged.

She stiffened. "What's that supposed to mean?"

"It means that you're so damned rational about everything, I sometimes wonder if you feel anything."

"I feel plenty. I just don't think it's necessary to share my emotions with everyone around me."

"I'm not everyone—I'm the man you're helping to raise

a child with," he pointed out, his voice tinged with frustration.

"I grew up in a home filled with drama," she told him. "And as if it wasn't enough that I had to live in it, I got to read about it in the headlines of the tabloids, so forgive me for wanting to spare Oliver that."

He knew some of her family history from Darren and Melissa—and yes, because he'd seen some of those same headlines—but he hadn't thought about how her parents' very public breakups and reconciliations had affected her. Until now.

"There are no photographers lurking in the bushes outside," he assured her.

She sat back in her chair and sighed, toying with Oliver's spoon as he played with a chunk of banana. "I know. Or at least the logical part of my brain does. And then I remember being blindsided when I walked out of school one day to find a reporter demanding to know how it felt to know that Peter Ross was claiming he wasn't my father."

"Jesus, Harper—I'm sorry."

She shrugged. "Apparently the tear-streaked face of a ten-year-old love child on the cover of a magazine helps to sell a lot of copies. Eventually, the test results proved that he *was* my father, but that wasn't worthy of mention."

No wonder she'd learned to hide her feelings.

Ryan was angry at the reporters who hadn't seen her as anything more than a juicy headline, sick for the child she'd been and frustrated that the woman she'd grown into was so determined to keep him at a distance. While he understood a little better now why she kept such a tight rein on her emotions, she needed to understand that they were a team and that they needed to work together to do what was best for Oliver. And it would be a lot easier to do that if he wasn't continuously running up against the walls she kept putting up between them. But her confession about her past gave him hope that she was starting to open up to him, at least a little.

Oliver had finished his snack, so Harper gave him his two-handled sippy cup. He raised it to his mouth, one-handed, and sucked back milk like a man taking a swig of beer.

Ryan couldn't help but smile, thinking about the countless brews that he'd tipped back over the years with Darren. "Like father, like son," he noted.

Harper's lips started to curve. Then her smile wobbled and her gaze shifted away.

He could guess what she was thinking, because his mind had gone in the same direction. His offhand comment had reminded both of them that the little boy wouldn't have the chance to learn anything else from either of his parents.

Grief made his chest feel tight, and that was before he saw the tears precariously balanced on Harper's bottom lashes.

Oh, crap.

He'd practically demanded proof of her emotions, but he hadn't wanted to see her cry.

What was he supposed to do now?

Ryan didn't have a lot of experience dealing with emotional females. It was rare for him to get so deeply involved with a woman that she'd feel comfortable crying on his shoulder, and even when he ended a relationship, he was careful to ensure there was no cause for tears.

Of course, this situation was completely different, and he knew he shouldn't be surprised by Harper's grief—it had been a hellish few weeks for both of them. Truthfully, he was a little surprised she hadn't broken down before now.

Not that she was breaking down now. Despite the shimmer of tears in her eyes and the quiver of her chin, she was valiantly fighting to hold it together. Obviously she didn't want him to see her cry any more than he wanted to see her cry.

Blindly, she unbuckled the belt around Oliver's tummy and lifted him from his high chair.

"Harper." He touched a hand to her shoulder, not sure what else he was supposed to say or do.

She shrugged off his touch. "Don't. Please."

"Don't what?" he asked helplessly.

"Don't be nice to me." It was as much a plea as a statement. "I'm barely holding on by a thread here, and if you show any understanding or compassion, you're going to have your arms full of blubbering female."

Then she thrust Oliver at him so his arms were full of squirming baby instead and fled from the room.

He stood there for a minute, not quite sure of his next move.

"Baff," Oliver said.

"You're right." He shifted the little guy onto his hip and headed toward the stairs, grateful for an assignment that he could handle. "Let's go get you into the bath."

A few days after she'd almost melted down in front of Ryan, Harper was feeling more in control of her emotions and a little more comfortable with Oliver. She was cutting Oliver's grilled cheese sandwich into strips so they were easier for him to pick up when her cell phone rang.

A quick glance at the display revealed that it was Adam McCready, the executive producer of *Coffee Time*. She ignored it. Whatever her boss's reason for calling, it probably wasn't as urgent as he thought.

As she reached into the cupboard for a sippy cup, she

felt Oliver tug on her skirt. He pointed to the jar on the counter. "Kee! Kee!"

"You can have a cookie after you have your sandwich," she promised, removing the lid to pour milk into his cup.

"Kee!" he insisted.

She scooped him up and settled him into his high chair, buckling the belt around his middle before sliding the tray into place. "Sandwich," she said. "Grilled cheese. Yum."

His arms stretched out in the direction of the cookie jar. "Um! Kee!"

She put the plate with his sandwich on his tray along with his drink.

Her phone had stopped ringing, but now the message light was blinking. She might have ignored the blinking as easily as the ringing except that it then chimed to indicate a text message from Diya.

HD canceled for 2morrow. Adam freaking. Thoughts 4 replacement?

HD was Holden Durrant—their spotlight guest, the one they'd been advertising all week.

She immediately called Durrant's agent and learned that the actor had the flu and was currently puking his guts out in a penthouse suite at the Courtland Hotel. Harper booked a new date for the following week and also secured a second appearance to coincide with May sweeps. Then she contacted Elaine Hiller—an up-and-coming local artist whose work had recently been exhibited at the New Morning Gallery in Asheville—and filled the vacant slot for the next day. After that she called Diya to give her an update, trusting that her assistant would inform the people in PR so they could run some last-minute promos about their new guest.

By the time that was all done, Oliver had finished his sandwich and his drink and was squirming to get out of his high chair. Harper cleared away his dishes, washed his face and hands, then set him on the floor to play with the box of plastic lids—one of his favorite kitchen toys— while she called Adam to personally assure the producer that the crisis had been averted.

Of course, he wasn't satisfied with that report but demanded to know when they were going to find time on the program for his wife's brother's daughter-in-law, who had recently published a children's book. Biting back her frustration, Harper went to the office to get her tablet so she could check the master schedule.

She'd just opened up the calendar when she heard a clatter, a crash and a scream. It all happened so fast she couldn't say which had actually come first. There was only one thought in her mind: *Oliver.*

She dropped the phone on top of the desk and raced back to the kitchen. The little boy was on the floor beside an overturned chair with pieces of broken cookie jar and scattered cookies on the floor around him.

But it was the blood mixed with streaming tears and dripping down his cheek that brought her racing heart to an abrupt stop.

Chapter Five

"Oh, sweetie." Harper carefully picked her way through the broken pottery to lift Oliver out of the mess.

"Kee?" he said, his lower lip trembling.

"I'm so sorry," she said, her own eyes filling with tears.

She grabbed her purse, shoved it inside the diaper bag, then slung that bag over her shoulder and carried Oliver out to her car.

She settled him into his seat, then dabbed at the blood on his cheek with a tissue, careful to avoid the cut on his face. She didn't know if there was any glass in the wound, but there sure was a lot of blood.

Twelve minutes later, she was checking in at the ER of Mercy Hospital.

Of course, Oliver's initial screams—probably a response triggered by more surprise than pain—had subsided. Now even his quiet sobs were fading and his tears had mostly dried. But when he tried to wipe the moisture from his cheek, he smeared blood on the back of his hand.

She gave her insurance information and Oliver's date of birth to the triage nurse. No, she wasn't his mother—both of his parents had died. Yes, she was his legal guardian. No, she didn't have any proof of her guardianship status. Yes, she was becoming increasingly frustrated by the endless questions with no evidence of a doctor anywhere in the vicinity.

"I have insurance. I have credit cards. I just want a doctor to look at him and fix him up," she implored the nurse.

"Please take a seat in the waiting area until you are called."

Harper held back a frustrated sigh—barely. "How long are we going to have to wait?"

"It shouldn't be too long."

Which, of course, wasn't any kind of answer at all.

She turned away, her own eyes brimming with tears of helplessness and frustration.

"Harper?"

She glanced up at the blurry figure in the white coat, then blinked and brought him into focus. It was Justin Garrett—Ryan's brother.

"What happened?" he asked her.

But when she opened her mouth to respond, she discovered that she couldn't force the words through the tightness in her throat.

Thankfully, Justin didn't seem to require a response. "I'll take them into exam room four," he told the triage nurse.

"But—"

"Dr. Seabrook is examining the elderly gentleman with chest pains in two and Dr. Wallace said she would take a look at the sebaceous cyst in three."

The nurse pursed her lips in silent disapproval, but she nodded and handed him the chart she'd prepared.

Justin led Harper into the exam room and gestured for her to sit on the bed. She did so, facing Oliver forward on her lap so that the doctor could evaluate his injury.

But Justin didn't seem in too much of a hurry as he pulled on a pair of sterile gloves. "Does Ryan know you're here?"

She shook her head, her stomach tensing at the thought of that inevitable conversation. "I didn't think to call him—or anyone. I just grabbed Oliver and came directly here."

"Why don't you give him a call now?" he suggested as he tore open a gauze pad and began to clean the blood from the baby's cheek.

"I know he went into the office for a meeting today—I don't think I should disturb him."

Justin paused to look at her. "You don't think he'll want to know what happened?"

"Of course," she agreed.

But the truth was, she'd hoped that a doctor—preferably someone other than Ryan's brother—would fix Oliver up so that Ryan would never need to know that she'd been negligent while the baby was in her care. Obviously that wasn't a possibility now.

While Justin cleaned the baby's cheek, she pulled her phone out and sent a quick text message to Ryan. If he was going to yell at her, she'd rather he did it in capital letters on a screen so that his brother didn't overhear.

"So what did happen?" Justin asked when she tucked her phone away again.

"He climbed onto a chair to get a cookie and pulled the whole jar off the counter."

"Did he get his cookie?"

"No. The jar broke along with all of the cookies in it."

"The tears are probably as much about missing out on his treat as the laceration."

"Kee?" Oliver said, giving credence to the doctor's assumption.

Justin smiled.

"Does he need stitches?" she asked him.

He shook his head. "The laceration isn't very deep."

"But there was so much blood."

"He's going to be fine." The doctor's tone was patiently reassuring as he dabbed something from a tube onto the baby's cheek.

But Harper wasn't so easily reassured. "Will he have a scar?"

"He might have a very faint line," he acknowledged. "But even if he does, it will hardly be noticeable."

"Hardly noticeable is still noticeable," she said.

"I know you're essentially a new mother, and it's natural for new mothers to worry about every little thing," Justin said. "But one of the things I've learned working in the ER is that bumps and bruises—and even sprains and breaks—happen. This might be your first hospital visit with him, but it won't be your last. And…" He paused, waiting for her to look at him. "…it wasn't your fault."

She didn't really believe him, but she nodded in acknowledgment of his statement.

Oliver, his thumb in his mouth now, snuggled against her breast.

"See? Even he knows it wasn't your fault."

Before she could respond to that, there was a knock at the door and then Ryan walked in. When the baby saw him, he straightened up, a drooly smile curving his lips.

"Hey, big guy—I didn't know you were planning a field trip to the ER today." His tone was deliberately light but the look he sent his brother was full of concern.

"He's fine," Justin said. "Just a minor laceration that we

closed up with Dermabond. It should heal up completely within a week."

"When you get home, you'll have to check his baby book to see if there's a page for 'First Trip to the Hospital,'" Ryan said to Harper.

She knew he was teasing—or she hoped he was. But his words unleashed a fresh wave of emotion—grief because this was only one of many firsts that her friend would not experience with her son, and guilt because, despite Justin's reassurances to the contrary, she couldn't help but feel responsible for Oliver's ordeal.

This time when the tears filled her eyes, she couldn't hold them back.

Ryan's panicked gaze shifted from Harper to his brother.

"Why don't I take Oliver to the cafeteria for the cookie he didn't get earlier?" Justin suggested.

"Kee!" Oliver agreed.

The doctor lifted the baby from Harper's arms and carried him out of the room.

She swiped at her tears, but her efforts were for naught.

"Do you want to tell me what this is about?" Ryan asked when they were alone in the exam room.

She shook her head and grabbed a tissue from the box on the counter as her tears continued to fall.

"You don't want to tell me, or you can't, because you can't cry and talk at the same time?"

She nodded.

"Okay, then." He hesitated for a moment, not certain how to console her—or even if she'd let him. But he reached out to circle her shoulders with his arms and draw her gently into his embrace. "Let it all out."

She offered only a token resistance, then tucked her face into his shoulder and sobbed as if she'd lost her best friend.

And she had.

Melissa and Darren had died less than a month earlier, but in that time, Ryan hadn't seen Harper shed a single tear. He couldn't say with any degree of certainty that she hadn't cried when she was alone, but he didn't think she had. She'd seemed to focus instead on the practicalities of what needed to be done without giving in to any emotion. He'd thought she didn't feel anything—obviously he'd been wrong. She'd just bottled it up inside, and now that the cork was out of the bottle, all of those emotions were pouring out.

When the storm of emotion finally subsided, he tipped her chin up to look into her eyes. They were still shimmering with moisture. Her lashes were wet and spiky, her cheeks streaked. Whatever makeup she'd put on that morning had been washed away—but she looked more real and more beautiful than he'd ever seen her, and it seemed not just natural but necessary to lower his head and kiss her.

Her breath caught when his lips brushed against hers, and she went completely still. But she didn't pull away, so he let himself linger, savoring her flavor, slowly deepening the kiss. Her hands lifted to his shoulders, almost tentatively, as her lips parted to welcome the leisurely exploration of his tongue.

She tasted sweet and hot and tantalizingly familiar. He'd kissed her before—and a whole lot more. And although the one night they'd spent together had been more than four years earlier, the memories flooded his brain and his body, making him ache and yearn for her.

Harper had called that night a mistake. He thought that assessment was rather harsh. In his opinion, falling into bed with her the night of Darren and Melissa's wedding had been an impulse—and probably one he should have resisted. But he couldn't regret it. He regretted only that the closeness they'd shared that night had somehow created greater distance between them the next day.

Four years ago, they'd been acquaintances with mutual friends. Now they were living together, sharing not just a home but custody of a little boy who needed both of them. Which meant that he couldn't afford to screw this up.

Slowly, reluctantly, he ended the kiss.

Harper blinked and drew in a breath, then exhaled, a little unsteadily. He knew just how she felt.

"That was...unexpected," she finally said.

"Yeah," he agreed. "And even though it probably wasn't very smart, I can't promise it won't happen again."

She opened her mouth, closed it without saying a word.

"If you've got something to say, say it."

"I should go get Oliver—he's overdue for his nap."

It was classic Harper—instead of dealing with messy and uncomfortable emotions, she'd rather pretend they didn't exist.

But he knew better now. He knew that beneath her cool, carefully composed facade was a warm and passionate woman who felt things deeply. That knowledge only made it harder for him to walk away.

And he needed to walk away—at least for now. They both needed some time to think about what was between them and to decide where they would go from here.

"Okay—I'll see you at home later."

Harper didn't walk out with him.

She needed a minute to herself, to settle her galloping heart and steady her shaky legs.

She wanted to dismiss what had happened as "just a kiss," but she knew there was no "just" about it. They'd been in the middle of an exam room in the ER department and she'd practically wrapped herself around him like a Tensor bandage.

She shook her head, as baffled as she was frustrated by the intensity of her response to him. The man only had to touch her and she'd practically melted into a puddle at his feet. And he knew it—dammit.

The attraction had always been there, but she'd managed to ignore it. Mostly. Of course, that was a lot easier to do when she'd crossed paths with him only a couple of times a year. Now that they were living together, it was a lot more difficult to disregard the tension between them. But she was determined to give it her best effort.

Her plan to act as if the kiss had never happened lasted only until Oliver was tucked into bed that night. When Ryan came downstairs, she was sitting on the sofa with her tablet, scanning reviews of Elaine Hiller's work and making notes for Caroline for the next day.

He sat beside her, angling himself against the arm of the chair so that he was facing her, and asked, "Are we ever going to talk about it?"

She considered her response as she copied and pasted a particularly favorable quote. "What is 'it'?" she finally said. "My negligent parenting or the kiss?"

"I was referring to the kiss," he admitted. "But before we get to that, you should know that what happened today is in no way a reflection of your parenting skills."

"How can you say that?"

"Because it's true. It could have happened when I was here—it could have happened with both of us here."

"But it didn't—it happened on my watch," she said, feeling not just responsible but miserable about it.

"Okay—let me ask you a question," he said. "Do you think my mom is a pretty good mother?"

"Your mom is amazing."

"So you wouldn't question her maternal skills?"

"Of course not."

"And yet I visited the hospital three times before my first birthday."

She eyed him skeptically. "Really?"

"The first time I was only seven months old—Justin swung a plastic bat and caught me above the eye." He touched his right eyebrow. "Right there—four stitches."

She leaned closer to look at the barely visible scar.

"When I was ten months old," he continued, "I swallowed one of Braden's marbles, apparently because he told me it was candy. Of course, I only have his word for that— it's not as if I actually remember what he said. And less than a month after that, I fell down the stairs and ended up with a concussion. That time, they had to keep me in the hospital overnight for observation."

"Your mother wasn't a bad mother—she just had rotten kids."

He chuckled. "There might be some truth to that. No doubt we kept her busy with countless cuts and bumps and bruises for a lot of years, during which time she was constantly worried that Family Services would show up at the door."

Her heart started to pound—she hadn't considered the possibility that anyone would think what happened was anything other than an accident. Yes, she should have been keeping an eye on Oliver, but it really was an accident.

The panic that was tying knots in her belly must have shown in her face, because Ryan said, "No one is going to call Family Services because Oliver pulled a cookie jar down off the counter."

She nodded, because she wanted to believe him.

"So let's move on to what happened after the cookie-jar caper."

"You kissed me," she said, determined to downplay the event.

"You kissed me back."

She could hardly deny it, so she tried to explain it instead. "It was an emotional moment. I was worried about Oliver and I felt responsible for what happened, and you were there for me—so...thank you."

His lips twitched, as if he was fighting against a smile. "Anytime."

Her cheeks flushed. "Actually, it's probably best if we agree that it won't happen again," she said. "Our situation is already complicated enough without adding sex to the equation."

"I don't disagree," he told her. "But I think that kiss today proved the attraction between us might be stronger than your determination to ignore it."

In the four weeks that had passed since they'd moved into the house to take care of Oliver, Harper and Ryan had made an effort to work together. But since the kiss they'd shared at the hospital, Harper had been trying to put as much distance between them as possible.

Bath time had been one of the fun tasks that they usually tackled together. The first time had been a wet adventure for all of them. Oliver loved splashing in the water, pushing his boats through the water and squeezing water out of his animal squirters—and onto Harper and Ryan. He was less enthralled with the washing of his hair and his body, so they'd learned to get that part over with first and let him enjoy some playtime after.

Tonight when she heard Ryan running Oliver's bath, she resisted the impulse to offer her help. Instead she stayed in the kitchen to clean up from the little boy's snack. Jam toast meant sticky fingerprints and crumbs all over his high chair.

She bypassed the dishwasher in favor of hand-washing the little boy's plate and cup, wiped down the high chair and scrubbed counters that were already spotless. She didn't realize how much time she'd spent on those tasks until Ryan returned with the baby clean and dressed in a dinosaur-print cotton sleeper.

"You're going to scrub the spots right out of the granite," he told her.

She folded the cloth over the towel rail under the sink and reached for the baby.

"Look at you all ready for night-nights," she said.

"Ni-ni," he agreed.

Her heart hitched inside her chest when he snuggled against her. And then, of course, he slipped his hand inside her shirt. Thankfully, Ryan, filling the baby's sippy cup with milk, didn't seem to notice.

"I think I'm going to sit outside with him for a little while tonight so that he can look at the stars," Harper said.

"I'll grab his blanket," Ryan said.

He did, and then opened the French doors that led out to the flagstone patio. It wasn't completely dark yet, but the solar garden lights that marked the edge of the patio glowed softly in the twilight.

Harper lowered herself onto one end of the wicker sectional. Ryan took the seat in the corner so that he could sit sideways, facing her.

"Do you remember when they bought this house?" he asked.

She nodded, smiling a little at the memory. "Melissa was so excited."

"I think Darren was more apprehensive than excited," Ryan told her. "He'd told me that they were looking for a starter home and somehow they ended up with a four-bedroom two-story overlooking a golf course—and he didn't even golf."

Melissa had confided to Harper that Darren didn't even want to go to the open house at first, because the property was outside the upper end of their price range. But she'd convinced him to take a look because it had everything they wanted: it was in a good neighborhood, close to all conveniences, within walking distance to the local schools and had a backyard big enough for all their children—because they planned to have at least three—to run and play.

"She wanted it more than he did," Harper acknowledged.

"And he would have given her anything to make her happy."

"The first time she brought me here, I could see why she fell in love with it." The inside of the house had been perfect. The four bedrooms included a fabulous master suite with a balcony overlooking the backyard; plus, there were three baths, a spacious eat-in kitchen with granite countertops and high-end appliances, a main-floor office/den, hardwood floors, cathedral ceilings and tons of windows to let in natural light.

"You obviously didn't see the backyard."

She chuckled softly in response to his dry tone. "Not until later."

"Because it was a disaster—and probably turned away so many prospective buyers that the sellers felt lucky to get Melissa and Darren's offer."

He was right—not only had the former owners not done anything with the green space, they'd completely neglected it so that it was overrun with weeds, except where their hounds had dug up the ground, and littered with dog feces.

Darren and Ryan had done the cleanup, shoveling poop

and hacking down weeds, while Melissa and Harper had toured local nurseries for plants and shrubs. She didn't know the names of even half of the flowers that she'd helped her friend put into the ground, but Melissa had diligently researched the soil and light to ensure a successful garden.

"It looks great now," she said, because it did.

Two years after the big cleanup, the garden was thriving. Tulips, daffodils and hyacinths were in bloom, adding bright splashes of red, yellow and purple to the landscape. As spring shifted to summer, other flowers and colors would take their places, but Melissa wouldn't be here to enjoy the prosperity of her garden.

Harper blinked back the tears that stung her eyes. "Tulips were her favorite flowers—she'd be thrilled to see them blooming."

"Of course they're blooming," Ryan said. "The bulbs were planted in well-fertilized soil."

She managed a smile. "They were happy here. Not for long enough—but they were happy here."

"So why do you look sad?"

"I got a call from Simon Moore today."

"Who?"

"The real estate agent."

Ryan frowned. "What did he want?"

"He wondered if we'd made any decisions about what we were going to do with the house."

"We're living in it."

"Right now," she agreed. "But I figured that was an interim arrangement."

"I figured it was a logical arrangement," he countered.

"We need to consider all of our options."

"What options? There's no room in my condo for even half of Oliver's stuff, so unless you've got more space than I do..." His words trailed off.

She shook her head. "I don't." And she'd already sublet her apartment, anyway. "But there's got to be some middle ground between a one-bedroom walk-up and a three-thousand-square-foot home on a half-acre lot."

"It's a lot of space," he agreed. "But it's a great neighborhood for a family—the neighborhood Melissa and Darren picked for their son."

"You're right," she agreed. "But Simon offered to come by on Saturday with some recent comparable sales to help us decide what we want to do."

"There's nothing to decide."

"Melissa and Darren named us guardians of their son and his property—jointly," she reminded him in what she thought was a very reasonable tone. "Which is why I'm trying to discuss this with you."

He set his jaw, an obvious sign that he was determined to be *un*reasonable. "No discussion necessary. We're not moving."

She sighed. "I just thought we should talk about the possibility."

"We just did," he said.

Chapter Six

Harper knew Ryan was right.

She also realized that she should have waited to introduce a discussion about the house until after they'd made a decision about day care for Oliver, because Ryan's refusal to move ahead on that issue was a clear indication of his unwillingness to upset the new status quo.

And it probably was too soon to be thinking about making any other major changes in Oliver's life, and moving was undoubtedly a major change. She didn't even mind admitting that Ryan was right in this instance—or she wouldn't have if he didn't act so authoritative and self-righteous.

Even so, she should have contacted Simon and told him not to come. But because she was mad at Ryan—or maybe just mad that he was right—she went through the motions with the real estate agent anyway.

Having sold the house to Melissa and Darren, Simon was familiar with the property and only wanted to do a quick walk-through. They finished up in the kitchen, where she offered him a cup of the coffee she'd made before he arrived. He accepted and they sat side by side at the island, drinking coffee and going over the sales reports on similar neighborhood properties that he'd generated for her.

"Thanks for this," she said, tapping a finger on top of the reports. "But I don't think we're ready to put the house on the market just yet."

"It's too soon," Simon guessed.

She nodded.

"I thought it probably was," he said. "But I didn't want you to miss out on the opportunity to list while the market was hot, as it is right now."

"We'll let you know if we change our minds," she assured him, grateful for his understanding.

"I'd appreciate it," he said, zipping up his portfolio. "So now that our business is concluded, how are you holding up?"

"Me?"

He smiled. "Yes, you."

"Oh, I'm doing okay." She sipped her coffee. "At least, I pretend that I am."

"You've been busy," he noted, and she knew he was referring to the pile of boxes in the master bedroom, designated for donation to Goodwill.

"It's hard to sit around surrounded by the memories. I find it helps to keep busy. Or if it doesn't help, it gives me a sense of accomplishment."

"You need a break," Simon told her.

"Maybe," she acknowledged, although she couldn't see one anywhere on the horizon.

"Why don't you let me take you out tonight?"

"Oh…um…" Through their tour of the house and conversation, she'd found him sincere and easy to talk to—

but she honestly hadn't perceived any signs of personal interest and wasn't sure how to reply now.

"We'll go somewhere with soft lighting and quiet music," he suggested. "Share some food and wine and get to know one another better."

"That's…tempting," she told him.

He smiled. "I'll pick you up at seven."

She shook her head. "I'm sorry. I appreciate the invitation, but I can't."

"Can't tonight or can't at all?"

"At all," she admitted. "Not right now, anyway."

He nodded and dropped a business card on top of the paperwork. "Call me if you change your mind."

"About selling, you mean?"

He smiled again and held her gaze. "About anything."

Ryan waited until she'd closed the door behind the real estate agent before he stepped into the kitchen to refill his own mug of coffee.

"You could have said yes," he told her. And then, in case she thought he meant about selling, he clarified, "About dinner, I mean."

She shook her head.

"Not your type?"

"I don't have a type. I also don't have a lot of free time, so the free time I do have I'd rather not waste making small talk with a guy who's silently assessing whether sex with me would be worth the effort of dinner and conversation."

"I don't have a high opinion of your real estate agent," he said. "But even I don't think his invitation warrants such a harsh indictment of the whole gender."

"My conclusion isn't without foundation," she assured him.

"Give me one example," he said.

Unfortunately, his request wasn't even a challenge. "Last

summer I let my assistant talk me into going out with her, her boyfriend and his brother. It was a disaster from the first. Tim—the brother—insisted on selecting the restaurant. He chose a new sushi restaurant downtown—and I don't like sushi.

"But Tim promised that I would like *this* sushi. And then he insisted on ordering for the whole group, bypassing the tamer options in favor of octopus, sea urchin and eel.

"Diya, obviously not having realized that her boyfriend's brother was such a Neanderthal, insisted that we stop at The Corner Deli on the way back because she knew I hadn't eaten anything. By that point, I wanted to go home more than I wanted food, but I went along so that she would stop fussing. And while I was waiting at the counter to place my order, Tim made a point of saying that he'd already forked over the cash for one meal and wasn't going to pay for my chicken wrap."

"Charming," Ryan noted drily.

She nodded. "And then, after we parted ways with Diya and her boyfriend, Tim actually thought I would invite him up to my condo for a drink.

"I said I was sorry—although the only thing I was sorry about was ever agreeing to meet the guy—but I didn't have anything to offer him to drink."

"How did he respond to that?" he asked.

"He shrugged and said, 'I don't mind skipping the drink and moving straight to the bedroom.'"

"You're kidding."

She shook her head. "I wish I was. And when I managed to overcome my bafflement and ask if he honestly expected me to sleep with him, he responded with, 'Why would you agree to go out with me if you didn't plan on having sex with me?'

"I explained that I thought the date was an opportunity

for us to get to know one another, to decide if we wanted to go on a second date, and he said he was 'too busy to play those kind of games' and if I wasn't interested, I should say so."

"I hope you told him you weren't interested."

"Very bluntly and succinctly."

"Never to see him again?"

"Never to see him again," she confirmed.

"We're not all like that," Ryan felt compelled to point out to her.

"I know. But the reality is that I don't have the time or energy for any romantic BS right now."

Her tone so perfectly matched her words, he couldn't help but smile. "That's no reason not to let a guy buy you dinner."

"You think I should have accepted Simon's invitation?"

"No," he admitted. "Because I think he's a weasel for trying to pick up a commission at a funeral. But if you'd said yes and left me on my own with Oliver tonight, then I wouldn't have to feel guilty about abandoning you when I go to the baseball game in Durham with my brother tomorrow afternoon."

"Why should you feel guilty?"

"Truthfully, I don't—because they're playing Charlotte and nothing could entice me to give those tickets away. But I feel like I should feel guilty."

She shook her head at that, but she was smiling. "No need," she assured him. "I think I can handle Oliver on my own for a few hours."

She was wrong.

Oliver was great when Ryan left—he stood at the door happily waving bye-bye and then toddled into the living room to play with his blocks. So Harper settled on the sofa with her tablet to review the schedule for the upcoming week. And as soon as Oliver saw that she was doing something other than paying attention to him, he abandoned his blocks in pursuit of her tablet.

She set her work aside and pulled him onto her lap to read him a book. He grew bored with that halfway through and wriggled away to return to his toys. She reached for the tablet again and was starting to get engrossed in the biography of Monday's feature guest—a psychiatrist who had written a book about the correlation between color and mood—when she caught movement out of the corner of her eye as Oliver slipped through the doorway.

She snagged him around the belly, making him giggle, and hauled him back into the living room. This time, she put him in his playpen—which was apparently his signal to scream as if he was being tortured.

"Just for an hour," she said, trying to bargain with the baby. "Just give me an hour to finish my prep and then we can go for a walk to the park."

Oliver refused to be bargained with. He didn't understand about future gratification—he wanted out of his playpen *now*. She put his blocks in the enclosure; he threw them out again. She gave him Woof, a plush beanbag puppy and his absolute favorite toy; he threw that, too.

Harper tried to ignore him. Some of the childcare guides advocated that strategy, but she quickly decided that the writers of those books must have had much quieter babies than Oliver. Of course, other books had said that a mother should never ignore a crying child. She'd read so many conflicting pieces of advice that she honestly wasn't sure what to believe, but she figured that ignoring his obviously temper-induced cries was okay because he could see that she was right there beside him.

Except that ignoring had absolutely no impact on his

temper or his tears, and after half an hour of rereading the same paragraph more times than she could count, she finally gave up, locked the screen of her tablet and lifted him into her arms.

Which was, of course, exactly what he wanted. And though she knew she wasn't supposed to let him "win," she didn't have the energy to battle with him. Instead she got him ready for a trip to the park. She wrestled the baby's feet into his athletic shoes, dabbed sunscreen on his face and neck and settled a baseball cap over his curls. It was only when she picked him up to put him in his stroller that she realized his diaper needed to be changed.

She sighed, tears of frustration burning behind her eyes. "Your mom made this all look so effortless."

He looked up at her with those heartbreakingly beautiful blue eyes that reminded her so much of her best friend. "Ma-ma?"

"Yes, I'm talking about your mama," she said as she pulled the change pad out of his diaper bag and settled him on it. "Your mama is no doubt looking down on us from heaven—and wondering how she ever thought I could handle the responsibility of her child."

The child, of course, had no reply to that.

She unsnapped his overalls and folded them out of the way, then unfastened the tabs of his diaper and pulled it away. As she was sliding the clean diaper under his bottom, a stream of something warm and wet hit her in the chest.

She swore—loudly.

But only inside her head.

Aloud she merely sighed.

"You'd think by now I would have learned."

Oliver babbled happily. Innocently.

She sighed again and finished securing the clean diaper,

then carried the baby upstairs with her so that she could change her clothes.

Half an hour after she'd decided to take him to the park, they were finally walking out the door.

She was both surprised and pleased when Kenna and Jacob showed up at the park a short while later.

"I hoped we would see you here," Kenna said. "Daniel's in Talladega this weekend and I'm finding myself in desperate need of adult conversation."

"Ryan's in Durham," Harper told her.

"Baseball game?"

She nodded. "I'm on my own with him for at least four hours every day, with—aside from one trip to the ER—no major difficulties. But today has been nothing *but* difficulties."

"Babies seem to instinctively know when you've been pushed to your limit—and then they push just a little bit further," Kenna agreed.

"I'm hoping to tire him out here so that when I put him down for his nap, he'll sleep until Ryan gets home."

"Good luck with that—Jacob naps on and off throughout the day, but never for more than half an hour at a time."

"How do you manage to get anything done?"

"It's a challenge," Kenna acknowledged. Then she shifted topic to ask, "Have you made any progress about day care for Oliver?"

"We're still evaluating options."

"Is that code for Ryan's still dragging his heels?"

"It is and he is," Harper confirmed. "Which I don't understand, because I know he's got to be as exhausted as I am."

She shook her head. "I honestly don't know how I'd manage to get out of bed in the morning if Ryan didn't handle the night shift."

"He gets up with Oliver every night?"

"Yes, he does."

"And I thought I was lucky that Daniel was willing to do every other night," Kenna said. "Of course, I still woke up when it was his turn, as I'm sure you do when Ryan gets up."

"No, I don't even hear him."

"Really? I wake up every time Daniel rolls over," Kenna admitted.

Harper felt her cheeks flush. "You think Ryan and I are sleeping together?"

"You're not?"

"No!"

"Whoops," Kenna said. "Sorry about that."

Harper's cheeks continued to burn, not just because of the assumption her friend had made but because she'd spent too much time alone in her bed dreaming about that exact scenario.

Kenna caught Jacob at the bottom of the toddler slide, then glanced over at her. "So now I'm wondering—why not?"

"Why not what?" she asked, desperately hoping that she'd missed a shift in the topic of conversation.

"Why aren't you letting Ryan keep you warm at night?"

"Because…" She wasn't entirely sure how to answer that question.

"Because?" the other woman prompted.

"Because that would be a really bad idea."

"Or a really good one," Kenna countered with a grin.

Harper just shook her head.

"You can't tell me you're not tempted," her new friend protested.

Unfortunately, Kenna was right—Harper couldn't say that she wasn't tempted, because it would be a lie. "I'm female and I'm breathing—of course I'm tempted," she admitted. "But we're both focused on doing what's best for Oliver."

The other woman offered Jacob a sippy cup when she saw him trying to get into the diaper bag. "Somehow I don't think 'what's best for Oliver' is the reason your cheeks are red."

"I'm not holding out on you," Harper insisted. "I just don't think it really meant anything."

"What 'it'?"

"He kissed me."

"Well, that's a start."

"And the finish," Harper insisted. "That was more than a week ago, and since then, nothing."

"Hmm," Kenna said. "Maybe he doesn't want to be perceived as taking advantage of the situation."

"And he probably realizes it would be awkward for Oliver to be caught in the middle when the relationship ends."

"Why are you assuming it would end?"

"Because that's what happens with relationships."

Kenna frowned. "After living with Ryan for more than a month, you should realize that he's not nearly as shallow as he lets people believe."

Harper had come to the same conclusion herself over the past several weeks. And the realization that he had more character and depth than she wanted to believe had unnerved her. It would be easier to fight her growing feelings if she could believe that he wasn't worth her time and attention.

Before she could respond, her cell phone started to ring. She pulled it out of an outside pocket of the diaper bag and looked at the screen.

"Excuse me," she said, "but I better take this."

"Of course," Kenna agreed, walking around to the other side of the climber to give her some privacy.

Harper connected the call, keeping an eye on Oliver as she talked. The conversation was brief and to the point, as were most of her conversations with Gayle Everton-Ross. Yes, she'd read the press release that had been emailed to her the day before; yes, she would look at the *Coffee Time* schedule and fit him in; yes, she would try to do it before Monday so that Gayle could schedule his other appearances.

"Sorry," Harper apologized to Kenna again when she tucked the phone away.

"You get business calls on Sundays, even?"

"Seven days a week," she confirmed. "But actually, that was my mother."

"And I thought I had an awkward relationship with mine," Kenna mused, making Harper laugh.

"My mother is also my dad's agent. He just got signed for a guest spot on *NCIS*, so she wants me to get him on *Coffee Time* before that."

"Ohmygod—I think I just put the pieces together," Kenna said. "Your father is Peter Ross?"

Harper nodded.

"He was my first crush," the other woman confided. "Not your father, really, but Brock Lawrie—his character on *The Light of Dawn*. When I was in ninth grade, some of the girls would sneak into the drama room where there was a TV so that we could watch during our lunch hour. When Brock first confessed his love for Lorelei…it was so…perfect."

Harper couldn't help but chuckle in response to Kenna's dramatic sigh.

"Sorry—I'm having a total fan-girl moment here," the other woman admitted.

"No need to apologize," Harper assured her. "The girls I went to high school with all watched it, too."

"But you didn't?"

She shook her head. "He might have been Brock Lawrie on TV, but he was still my dad, and watching him kiss other women on-screen was just too weird."

"I guess it would be," Kenna agreed. "I still watch *The Light of Dawn* sometimes—and Brock and Lorelei still have some powerful chemistry."

"Which is probably why my mother hates that story line."

"It must be hard—to be married to a man who's famous for seducing women in front of the camera."

Harper sighed. "It wouldn't be nearly so hard if it was just in front of the camera."

Aubrey Renforth had made a lot of mistakes in her life but none that she regretted more right now than walking away from her family.

For a long time, she'd held her parents and her brother responsible for the estrangement. After all, they were the ones who had refused to come to the wedding, insisting that she was too young to get married—and that Jeremy was too old for her.

So she'd built her own life with her husband, they'd created their own family, and she trusted that she'd followed the path she'd been meant to follow. Her only connection to the life she'd left behind was Tracy Blaine, her best friend since sixth grade.

Over the years, Aubrey and Tracy had kept in touch regularly if not frequently. And though Aubrey was certain she didn't miss anyone that she'd left behind, she looked forward to Tracy's emails and the glimpses of the town that had once been her home.

It was through her friend that she'd learned about Darren's wedding to Melissa and, less than a year after that, her father's stroke and her mother's subsequent decision to move them both into an assisted-living facility. Two years later, Tracy had sent her a link to Oliver's birth announcement in the online version of the local paper. Aubrey printed the notice and kept it safe inside her jewelry box.

Throughout all the years and those major events, she'd never once gone back to Charisma—she'd never wanted to. While the aging of her parents was sad, it was also inevitable; the deaths of her brother and his wife were shocking and devastating. But it was her concern for their child—the nephew she'd never even met—that propelled her into action and brought her to where she was now.

24 Springhill Garden.

She looked at the address on the square of paper in her hand and matched it to the number on the front of the house. Then she tucked the note back into her pocket and pressed the bell. She heard the faint echo of its chime through the door and clutched the handle of her purse with both hands.

The woman who answered the door was younger than Aubrey had expected and quite attractive, with warm brown eyes and a quick smile.

"Can I help you?"

She held out her hand. "I'm Aubrey Renforth—Darren's sister."

"Oh." The dark eyes widened in evident surprise but she took the proffered hand automatically. "I'm Harper Ross—a friend of Darren and Melissa's. Are you here…? I mean… do you know…about the accident?"

"I was away for a few weeks, but I came as soon as I heard."

"And I guess you didn't stop by to stand on the porch,"

Harper said, stepping back from the door so that Aubrey could enter the spacious foyer.

"Can I get you something to drink?" she asked, leading the way to the kitchen. She opened the fridge, peeked inside. "I've got lemonade and sweet tea."

"No, thank you."

"I'm so sorry you weren't informed of the arrangements," Harper said, sounding both sympathetic and sincerely apologetic as she took a seat at the granite island and gestured for Aubrey to do the same. "Unfortunately, no one knew how to get in touch with you."

She dropped her gaze. "Regrettably, my brother and I lost touch quite a few years back."

"I'm sorry for your loss."

Aubrey nodded in acknowledgment of her sympathy. "But in the end, no matter what has come before, blood is thicker than water, isn't it?"

"You're here to see Oliver," the other woman guessed.

"I think that would be a good start."

Chapter Seven

Harper wasn't sure what to make of that cryptic response. In any event—blood relative or not—she wanted to know a little bit more about this woman before she introduced her to Oliver.

She opened the cupboard and took out two glasses, filled them with sweet tea. Aubrey had said she didn't want anything, but Harper needed a minute to gather her thoughts and pouring the drinks bought her that time.

"Where is my nephew?" the visitor asked, obviously impatient to meet him.

"Napping."

"Oh." Aubrey folded her hands on the counter.

Harper noted the rings on her finger: a wide gold wedding band and an engagement ring with a cluster of diamonds. Her fingers were thin, delicate, her skin so pale that her veins were visible beneath the surface.

Darren had been a big man—broad shouldered and solidly built, and at first glance, Harper would never have believed they were siblings. But there was some resemblance between Oliver and this woman, evident in the shape of their eyes if not the color—Oliver had inherited the deep clear blue from his mother—and the subtle dent in the middle of their chins.

"I'm sure you can appreciate that this has been an incredibly difficult time for Oliver. For all of us, really."

"I'm grieving, too," Aubrey told her.

"I know. But I have to ask—when did you last see your brother?"

The other woman dropped her gaze. "Eighteen years ago," she admitted. "I was only eighteen myself when I left Charisma to go to Presbyterian College in South Carolina. That's where I met Jeremy, and we fell in love. I brought him home at Thanksgiving to meet my family, but he was older—and divorced—and it was obvious to both of us that my parents didn't approve of our relationship.

"It was only a few weeks after the New Year that Jeremy was offered a job in Washington, and he asked me to go with him. My parents forbade me to go, but I was a legal adult and didn't need their permission and I told them so. My mother said that if I went, I shouldn't bother to come back. So I didn't."

Harper sipped her tea. "Eighteen years is a long time to be out of touch with family."

"It is," Aubrey agreed, sounding genuinely regretful. "And I never planned to be gone so long—the years just seemed to slip away."

"Are you still living in Washington?"

"No. We moved to Virginia about five years ago. We live just outside Martinsville now."

Harper wondered how it was that this woman had been living less than a hundred miles away and never made the effort to breach that distance to visit her brother and his family. Even more concerning was why she'd made the effort now.

Aubrey rubbed at the condensation on the outside of her glass. "When can I see him—Oliver?"

"He'll be waking up shortly."

As if on cue, Harper heard through the baby monitor the telltale sounds of Oliver stirring in his crib. Thankfully, he awakened from his naps much more gradually and peacefully than he awakened in the night.

"That's him, isn't it?" Aubrey asked eagerly.

Harper understood that the other woman was anxious to finally meet her nephew, and while she knew that she had no right or reason to refuse, she was wary.

But she led the way to the baby's room, where Oliver was playing in his crib, cooing and babbling nonsense. When she peeked in through the doorway, she saw he was sitting up in his crib and chewing on one of the ears of his beanbag puppy, but he dropped the toy when he saw her.

He grasped the bars of the crib and hauled himself up, bouncing excitedly on the springy mattress. "Up-up-up."

Harper smiled. "Yes, we'll get you up."

Then his gaze shifted past her to Aubrey, and the wide smile that creased his face slipped a little. He'd never shown any hesitation about meeting new people, but he was a little wary now.

"This is your aunt Aubrey," Harper told him. "Your daddy's sister."

Oliver's smile returned in full force. "Da-da-da."

Harper gently brushed a soft curl off his forehead. "You're a clever boy, aren't you?"

"Da-da-da," he repeated.

"Can I?" Aubrey asked, indicating that she wanted to pick him up.

Harper noted that Oliver looked more curious than uncertain now, so she shrugged and stepped back from the crib. "Sure."

"Hello, Oliver." Tears shone in the other woman's eyes as she approached the baby. "Did you have a good nap?"

"Up-up-up," Oliver demanded.

Aubrey smiled as she lifted him from his crib. "You're a big boy, aren't you? Built like your daddy."

"Da-da-da."

His aunt put a hand under his bottom to support him. "I think his diaper needs changing."

"No doubt," she agreed, reaching for the baby.

"I don't mind doing it," Aubrey said, already moving toward the changing table.

"Okay," Harper reluctantly agreed.

She hovered behind Aubrey as she gently laid the baby down on the padded surface. There was no reason to think the other woman wasn't competent, but something about her proprietary behavior made Harper uneasy.

Aubrey completed the diaper change quickly and effortlessly. She even remembered to keep the little boy covered so that the cool air didn't trigger an automatic response. It had taken Harper a long time and far too many accidents before she remembered to have the clean diaper ready prior to removing the dirty one.

"You obviously have a lot of experience at that," she commented.

"I love babies," Aubrey told her.

"Do you have any children of your own?"

Oliver's aunt shook her head as she dropped the dirty diaper into the bin beside the table. "Jeremy—my husband—has four from his first marriage, but we don't have any together."

Her matter-of-fact tone made it difficult for Harper to

decipher how she felt about her childless status. But she suspected, based on her sudden appearance in Oliver's life, that she wished her situation was different.

"It was a shock to learn that my baby brother had a baby of his own," Aubrey continued.

"But you never wanted to see Oliver—until now?"

"I wanted to—I just didn't know how to make it happen." The other woman's eyes filled with tears. "Now it's too late to reconcile with Darren, but it's not too late to do the right thing for his son." She snapped his pants up and lifted Oliver into her arms again.

"What is it that you think is the right thing for his son?" Harper asked her.

"To take him home with me so that he can be raised by family."

"I hope that's when you showed her the door," Ryan said when Harper recounted the story of Aubrey's visit for him over dinner that night.

"No, but I did show her the court order legalizing our guardianship and assured her that we were going to honor Melissa and Darren's wishes by raising Oliver together."

"How did she respond to that?"

"She didn't seem very pleased," Harper admitted. "She kept insisting that he should be with family."

"She didn't have any contact with her brother in all the years that I knew him and suddenly she's all about family?"

Harper briefly summarized Aubrey's explanation for the estrangement.

"Almost two decades is a long time to hold a grudge," he commented.

She nodded. "Too often people put things off until another day, only to find that they've missed their chance.

I think she wanted to reconnect with her brother and as-sumed it would happen someday, but now it's too late, so she's reaching out to Oliver instead."

"You don't think it's suspicious that she suddenly de-cided to come back now, after so many years?"

"No," she said again. "I mean, it makes sense that she'd want to reach out upon hearing about her brother's death."

"Maybe," he acknowledged. "Or maybe she wanted to see if there was any kind of inheritance."

"If that was her intention, she'll be disappointed, be-cause everything Darren and Melissa had is in trust for Oliver."

"And who controls that trust?"

She frowned at the question. "We do."

"Because we're his guardians," he pointed out.

"You really think Darren's estranged sister came here upon hearing the news of her brother's death for the pur-pose of ascertaining if he'd left any money and—if he did—to offer to take care of his orphaned son to get her hands on that money?"

"I don't know what to think," Ryan admitted. "I'd almost forgotten that Darren even had a sister until Oliver was born. When he asked me to be the little guy's godfather, I suggested that he might want to choose someone from his family, and he said there was just his sister—and no."

"That seems an odd response," Harper noted.

He nodded. "Of course, I didn't push for more of an explanation, because I figured if there was something he wanted me to know, he'd tell me." He scrubbed his hands over his face, frustrated that he wouldn't ever know now what his friend had meant.

And now it was too late. All he could do was honor Darren's wishes to care for Oliver, and that was what he intended to do.

* * *

The following Saturday afternoon, Harper was in the cereal aisle of the grocery store comparing the nutritional labels of Multi-Grain Cheerios, which was her usual purchase, and Honey Nut Cheerios, Ryan's request, when Fran Murphy—a retired school bus driver who lived down the street—drew her cart up alongside Harper's.

"Hello, Harper."

"Hi, Mrs. Murphy."

The older woman reached past her to take a box of Apple Cinnamon Cheerios from the shelf.

After depositing the cereal in her basket, she gestured to the package of disposable diapers in Harper's. "You know, my daughter-in-law buys all of her baby supplies at the supercenter in Chapel Hill—she says that she gets twice as many diapers for the same price there."

"That's quite a distance to go just to save a few dollars on diapers."

"Not just diapers," Fran said. "Baby wipes and formula and powder and shampoo."

"I'll keep that in mind the next time I'm out that way," Harper promised.

Mrs. Murphy nodded, apparently satisfied with that response. "How is young Oliver?"

"He's doing okay."

"Did you know I used to babysit sometimes?" Fran asked. "When Melissa and Darren wanted to go out to see a movie or have a romantic meal somewhere, they'd give me a call to look after the baby."

Harper nodded. "Melissa told me how much she appreciated knowing Oliver was in good hands when she wanted a bit of a break."

"Caring for a baby is a full-time job, as I'm sure you now realize."

"I do," she agreed. "Which is why I'm shopping for groceries and Oliver is home with Ryan."

The other woman chuckled. "Well, if you and Ryan ever want to get out together, I'd be happy to sit with the little one."

"Oh. Um…thank you, but I don't think that will be necessary."

"A night out might be welcome even if it's not necessary."

Harper opened her mouth to respond, then closed it again. She got the impression that the older woman thought her relationship with Ryan was something more than it was, and it was instinctive to want to clarify the situation for her. But in the end, she just wanted to get her groceries and get home.

"You'll remember what I said about calling me to babysit if ever you need me?" Fran prompted.

"I will," Harper promised.

"Then I'll look forward to hearing from you."

Harper thanked her again and started to push her cart forward as Mrs. Murphy continued the opposite way. She was nearly at the end of the aisle before she realized that she hadn't decided which cereal to buy. She backtracked and put both boxes in her cart.

When Harper got home from the grocery store, Ryan had Oliver secured in his high chair playing with the homemade dough she'd made for him, so he helped her unpack and put away the groceries.

Shopping had been much simpler when he was just feeding himself—mostly from the frozen-food section. He'd bought a lot of meals that could be taken out of a box and put directly into the microwave. Easy cooking and easier cleanup.

Harper was a fan of fresh fruits and vegetables—and salad. He'd never known anyone who ate as much salad as she did.

He'd brought home a couple of salted caramel brownies from The Sweet Spot one day, just because he'd been near the bakery and decided that he was in the mood for something sweet. Harper had looked at the brownies with unmistakable longing—and then at him as if he was the devil for putting temptation in her path.

And he knew that she had been tempted—but she'd resisted.

He'd eaten both of them for dessert that night; she'd had a bowl of strawberries.

"I got chicken for dinner," Harper said. "Do you want to grill it or should I make a stir-fry?"

Over the past few weeks, they'd fallen into a routine of making and eating dinner together. It wasn't anything they'd planned—it had just happened that way—so it hadn't occurred to him to tell her that he had other plans.

"Actually...I have a...um...date tonight," he told her now.

"Oh." Harper put the package of chicken breasts in the refrigerator. "Okay."

"I'm sorry—I should have said something earlier."

"You don't have to clear your schedule with me," she assured him.

"I didn't because, honestly, I forgot about it until Whitney texted me half an hour ago."

"It's okay," she said again, putting a rack of ribs in the freezer. "Have a good time."

Her tone was neutral—as if she honestly didn't care that he was going out or even whom he was going with. And she probably didn't. She'd made it more than clear four years ago that the one night they'd spent together would not be repeated. And one sizzling kiss aside, there had been absolutely no indication that her opinion on the matter had changed since then.

But it felt strange to Ryan, to be getting ready to go out with Whitney when the woman he really wanted was under the same roof.

He'd considered canceling his date. In fact, he'd picked up his phone at least half a dozen times to do just that. But for what purpose? So that he could spend another night at home, in the same room with Harper but not actually with her? Not exactly his idea of a good time.

Whitney offered at least the possibility of a good time. A few hours out of the house in the company of a beautiful, interesting woman he'd met a couple of months earlier on a flight from Raleigh to Philadelphia.

He'd been on his way to a business meeting; she'd been heading to West Chester for her sister's wedding. They'd had coffee together during the layover in Washington and chatted throughout the rest of the flight. As a single woman six years older than the bride, Whitney had been bracing herself for the false sympathies of her numerous cousins over her unmarried status.

After all, she was—she'd whispered the confession— almost twenty-eight years old and, according to her mother, who had married at nineteen, on the verge of spinsterhood. But she'd assured Ryan that she wasn't in any hurry to get married or settle down—she was enjoying her life too much to want to change it.

And in the end, that was why he didn't cancel. He just wanted to spend some time with someone who had no expectations of anything from him. When he arrived to pick her up, he was glad that he hadn't changed their plans. She'd obviously gone to some effort to get ready for their date and was wearing a strapless red dress that clung to her curves—and she had some very nice curves.

She was undoubtedly an attractive woman, with blunt-cut blond hair and clear green eyes, and if he passed her on the street, he'd probably do a double take. But aside from that initial and basic stirring of male appreciation, he felt nothing. No zing of heat, no sizzle of desire.

Instead he found himself thinking that she was taller than Harper, a little curvier than Harper, more outgoing than Harper, and he grew frustrated with himself for the continuous comparisons. As he drove toward Valentino's for their eight o'clock reservation, he suspected that he was wasting her time as well as his own. But she was easy to talk to and he was hungry, so he ignored his misgivings and made an effort to enjoy the evening.

She ordered the portobello mushroom ravioli in a creamy sun-dried tomato sauce, he opted for the chicken marsala, and they shared a bottle of sauvignon blanc.

Conversation was casual throughout the meal. She regaled him with stories of her sister's wedding that had him chuckling along with her. He told her about Oliver and his current living arrangement, wanting to be up front with her because it had turned out to be such an issue with Bethany. Whitney didn't seem concerned.

As she sipped her wine, she told him about her job as a yoga instructor and how years of training and discipline ensured that her body could bend in ways he probably couldn't even imagine. The smile that accompanied the claim suggested that she wanted him to imagine, but he really wasn't tempted by the implicit invitation.

"Is everything okay?" Whitney asked when he failed to respond to her teasing comment. "You seem a little… distracted."

"Sorry. I was thinking about Oliver."

She winced. "Am I that boring?"

"Of course not," he denied. "It's just that he has specific routines before bed, to help him settle down, and I'm usually the one who gives him his bath. I'm just a little worried that he'll give Harper a hard time."

"I'm sure they're fine." She reached across the table and brushed her fingertips over his wrist. "But if you want, maybe we could go back to my place and you could tuck me in."

She was a beautiful, sexy woman and she'd been sending him clear signals all night. He wasn't oblivious. Unfortunately, he also wasn't the least bit tempted. Because while Whitney was undoubtedly attractive, he was not attracted.

He couldn't stop thinking about Harper, wanting Harper. Despite the fact that she'd given no indication that she felt the same way and all kinds of hints to the contrary, he knew he couldn't be with one woman when he was preoccupied by thoughts of another.

"I'm sorry," he said. "There's too much going on in my life to start a relationship right now."

"Who said anything about a relationship?" she challenged. "I just want to have a good time."

Which he didn't need to be a linguistics expert to know translated into simple no-strings sex. A one-night stand. He hadn't had a one-night stand since…Harper.

What was it about the woman that all of his thoughts seemed to circle back to her? Was it a natural consequence of their circumstances—living together and raising a child together? Or was it more than that? Because even though he knew a relationship between them would be messy and complicated, she was the only one he wanted.

"Ryan?" Whitney prompted.

"Let me pay the bill and I'll take you home."

She smiled. "I'm just going to make a quick trip to the ladies' room to freshen up."

Ryan signaled for the bill, then pulled out his phone and sent a quick text to Harper.

how's everything there?

Good.

oliver settling down ok?

He's already asleep.

He hadn't expected that and was, perhaps, a little disappointed that he obviously wasn't needed at home.

Is everything okay there? she prompted.

great

He sent the single-word message, then followed up with another.

i might be late

No problem.

He figured she couldn't make it any more obvious that she didn't want the same thing he did.

He signed the credit card receipt and tucked his phone away again as Whitney came back to the table. "Let's go."

Chapter Eight

Harper stared at the message that Ryan had sent and wondered why the man couldn't seem to capitalize or punctuate his text messages.

i might be late

It was laziness, she decided, annoyed that he couldn't be bothered to make an effort. Or maybe she was more annoyed by the content of the message than the delivery, because the brief statement confirmed that he was having a great time on his date with Whitney and wasn't in any hurry to come home.

She was annoyed, too, with her own response.

No problem.

But what other response could she have given? What could she have said? She didn't want to admit that she still struggled when she was on her own with Oliver, and she definitely didn't want to admit—even to herself—that the idea of Ryan with another woman drove her insane.

Which was crazy, because she didn't want him. Or—as he'd pointed out—she did want him, but she didn't want to want him. And if she hadn't had enough reasons four years ago, their current situation added another.

And her current situation was pacing the floor with an unhappy baby.

"You said he was sleeping."

She jolted at the sound of his voice from the doorway. "And you said you were going to be late," she reminded him, shifting Oliver to her other shoulder.

He shrugged. "Change of plans."

"Well, Oliver *was* asleep," she said, then sighed. "He woke up when I put him in his crib and hasn't stopped crying since."

"Do you want me to take him?"

She responded by transferring the little boy to his arms.

Of course, as soon as she did so, Oliver drew in a long shuddery breath and stopped crying.

She shook her head. "Sometimes I wonder why I'm even here."

Ryan rubbed Oliver's back as the baby snuggled against his shoulder. "Because he needs you."

"Apparently he needs *you*."

"And when you're not here, he's just as fussy for me," Ryan told her. "He needs both of us."

She crouched down to pick the scattered toys up off the floor. "I just thought I'd be better at this by now."

"You're doing great. He just needs some time to get used to the new status quo."

"How much time?" she wondered.

"I don't think there's a definitive answer to that," he

said. "But you should probably count on the three of us being together for the next eighteen years or so."

"I hope it won't take that long for him to learn to put himself to sleep."

"It wouldn't really be so bad, would it—for the three of us to be a family?"

"Of course not," she said. "It's just that I had no plans for a family—at least not at this stage in my life."

"So when?"

"When I was where I want to be with my career."

"Where's that?" he asked curiously.

"Executive producer."

"Will you really be satisfied with that? Or will that just become a stepping-stone to something else?"

"What are you talking about?"

He shrugged. "It seems to me that you're always looking for something more or better than what you have."

"I'm not *always*," she denied.

"What about the night of Darren and Melissa's wedding?"

She froze. "What about it?"

"I thought we were pretty spectacular together that night."

"I—I don't remember."

It was a blatant lie, of course, and the smile that curved his lips confirmed he knew it, even before he whispered "Liar" close to her ear, then nibbled gently on her lobe.

Her eyes instinctively closed and a low moan sounded deep in her throat.

"Do you remember how many times I made you come that night?"

"No," she said, which wasn't a lie, because she'd lost count. The things he'd done to her body, the way he'd touched her, with his hands and his lips, had given her mindless, endless pleasure.

"Neither do I," he admitted. "But I never got tired of hearing you scream."

She started up the stairs. "It was a long time ago."

"You don't think I could make you scream again?" Ryan asked, following right behind her.

"I think Oliver does all the screaming we need in this house." She turned on the light in the baby's room, pulled back the sheet on his bed so that Ryan could put him down.

He did so—and they held their collective breath for a moment, waiting to ensure that he was really asleep.

Ryan nodded and she gently laid the sheet on the baby, then turned toward the doorway. She started past him, but he caught her around the waist and pulled her close.

Her breath caught; his teasing smile faded; and the air fairly crackled with sexual energy. She lifted her hands to his chest, to keep him at a distance. He caught them with his own, held her close.

"Whitney invited me back to her place tonight," he told her.

"So why didn't you go?" she challenged.

He held her gaze. "Because I couldn't be with her while I was thinking of you."

"Oh."

"I didn't even kiss her."

She didn't ask why—she didn't want to hear him say that he wanted to kiss her. Because she was afraid that if he did, she'd invite him to do so.

But he didn't seem to expect a response—or an invitation.

He lowered his head and covered her lips with his.

And just like the last time, just like the first time, she melted. Not just into the kiss but into him. His mouth moved over hers, boldly, confidently, not just coaxing but demanding a response.

She gave it willingly. She kissed him back until her heart was pounding and her head was spinning and her body was pressing against his, silently begging for more. A lot more.

But once again, he drew back, exhaling an unsteady breath as he leaned his forehead against hers.

"I wanted you the first time I saw you," he told her. "The night we met at Topaz."

She remembered that night, of course, and her own unexpected and intense reaction to meeting her best friend's boyfriend's best friend for the first time. She'd worried that her friend was playing matchmaker. Then she'd seen Ryan sitting beside Darren and all of her misgivings had dissipated. Because there was no way a guy who looked like that needed to be set up with anyone. And if by chance she was wrong and it was a setup, well, how could she object to being set up with a guy who looked like that?

It was an undeniably shallow reaction, but she'd been twenty-one years old and not particularly interested in depth. She had, however, been interested in ambition, and the gorgeous, sexy college student had been too laid-back. More interested in heli-skiing and rock climbing and diving than building a career.

He'd said nothing to defend himself or his character. In fact, he'd told her that he had no interest in a woman who was so tightly wound up she practically vibrated—no matter how sexy she was. This matter-of-fact acknowledgment of his attraction had taken her aback.

And aroused her. Not that she'd been willing to admit the fact—and definitely not to *him*. But the chemistry between them had simmered from that first night and for the next two and a half years—until it finally boiled over the night of the wedding.

"I still want you," he said now. "But the next move is yours."

The next move is yours.

She wasn't sure if his words were intended as a reprieve or a challenge, but she had other worries—such as Oliver starting day care on Tuesday.

Melissa had taken a leave of absence from her job a few weeks before Oliver was born and, at the time of the accident that took her life, had not yet decided if and when she would go back to work. For the whole of his life to that point, she'd been her son's primary caregiver, so day care would be a big change for him.

Harper agreed with Ryan that the little boy should be eased into the new environment. So while Oliver would be going to day care, it would be only part-time in the beginning. A few hours a day three days a week.

Harper had done her research, arguing that children who went to day care had better socialization skills and fewer illnesses when they started school. Ryan wasn't convinced. In the end, it was a simple logistical issue—he couldn't effectively do his job if he wasn't in the office on a more regular basis.

They'd spent a lot of time discussing the pros and the cons, visiting facilities and meeting the caregivers. When they finally made their decision, she was confident it was the right one. But the night before Oliver's first day, she found herself wondering if she'd pushed for it to happen too soon, and she continued to hold on to him long after he'd fallen asleep in her arms.

Around nine o'clock Ryan came upstairs. "What's the matter?"

She got up from the rocking chair and finally put the baby in his crib. "I'm having second thoughts about Oliver starting day care tomorrow," she admitted.

To his credit, he didn't say "I told you so."

To her surprise, he said, "He's going to be fine."

She nodded, because after advocating in favor of putting him in day care for weeks, she could hardly argue against it now.

"It's only a few hours," he reminded her. "I'm going to drop him off at eight thirty and pick him up at eleven thirty."

They'd agreed that they would ease the little boy into the new routine, starting with three hours a day three days a week. When he was accustomed to that and actually looking forward to going—which she hoped would happen— they would add an hour at a time until he was going full days three days a week.

The morning that Ryan was scheduled to take Oliver to the Wee Watch Childcare Center, she found herself constantly glancing at her watch. At seven o'clock, she wondered if they were awake. At seven thirty, she considered calling to make sure they were up. At seven forty-five, she speculated about what Ryan was feeding the little boy for breakfast. At eight o'clock, she knew they would be getting ready to leave the house. By nine thirty, Diya had threatened to take her watch to ensure that she focused on *Coffee Time.*

When the show was finished, she raced through the usual wrap-up to get home to hear about Oliver's first day at Wee Watch.

He was playing with his blocks when she walked in the door, but he abandoned them to rush over and give her a big hug. She hugged him back, relieved to see that he'd survived his first day apparently unscathed.

"You're home early," Ryan noted.

"A little," she said, unwilling to admit that she'd rushed for any particular reason. "How was Oliver when you took him to day care today?"

"Good."

She eyed him suspiciously. "Really? No clinging? No crying?"

"Just a little, but the childcare worker promised a lollipop if I'd let go."

"Ha-ha."

"Okay, Oliver cried, too," Ryan admitted. "Huge sobs and fat tears, and if I didn't have that meeting, I'm not sure I would have been able to walk away."

"How was he when you went back to pick him up?"

"Fine. He was sitting in one of those little chairs at a round table eating cubes of cheese and raisins, and when I told him it was time to go, he didn't want to leave."

She frowned. "I thought snack time was ten o'clock."

Ryan didn't say anything.

"What time did you pick him up?"

He sighed. "It was ten o'clock."

"Why?"

"Because I felt so guilty for leaving him there when he was obviously so unhappy."

"So he was at day care for a whole hour and a half?"

"We both agreed that it would be best to ease him into a new routine," he reminded her.

"Which is why he was supposed to start with three hours," she reminded him.

"We'll try for three hours tomorrow."

"Try?"

"How was your day?" he asked, in an obvious effort to shift the conversation.

"Good. We had Holden Durrant on the show today, and 'Tuesday Trivia.'"

"I'm glad you weren't worried about Oliver."

She narrowed her gaze on him. "They told you I called."

"Apparently three times."

"Okay, yes," she admitted. "I just wanted to make sure he was doing okay."

"*Three* times," he said again.

"*You* picked him up early."

"My meeting finished early," he said. "It didn't make sense to come home and then go back out to pick him up later."

She sighed. "Are we in danger of becoming helicopter parents that hover over their kids all of the time? Or do you think even normal parents try to shield their children from difficult situations?"

"I don't know," he said. "But that's a scary thought."

"That we're parents?"

He smiled as he shook his head. "That we're normal."

When Ryan finally got to his office later that afternoon, there was a brisk knock on his door and then his cousin Nathan poked his head through. "Are you busy?"

"I haven't been here long enough to get busy," Ryan admitted. "What's up?"

"I just wanted to check in to see how everything was going."

"Here or at home?"

"Either or," his cousin said. "I know you've adjusted your work schedule to help with the baby."

"Poor kid, huh?"

Nate grinned. "I wasn't going to say it."

Ryan's answering smile quickly faded. "It really does

suck. I mean, I think we're doing okay—me and Harper—but we're not Oliver's parents."

"One of the things I've learned, being with Allison and Dylan, is that biology is only one part of the equation. As long as you love the kid—and it seems pretty obvious that you do—you'll figure things out."

"I hope so."

"So how's everything else?"

"Work is fine. I've managed to keep on top of most things despite the hours I'm not in the office."

"That's great, but not what I was referring to."

Ryan's brows lifted. "What else is there?"

"The fact that you're living with a woman for the first time in your life."

"We're not living together," he denied. "Okay—we are *living* together, but we're not living *together*."

Nate smirked. "Glad you cleared that up."

"You know what I mean."

"I guess I do. I just thought…maybe…" His words trailed off suggestively.

"No," Ryan said firmly.

"Are you still seeing Bethany, then?"

He shook his head.

"Why not?"

"She wasn't happy to learn that I would be sharing a house and childcare responsibilities with another woman and accused me of choosing Harper over her."

"Did you?"

He shook his head. "Harper is so not my type."

"I saw her at the funeral," Nate reminded him. "Since when is your type not brunette and beautiful?"

"Uptight is not my type," Ryan clarified.

"She didn't seem uptight to me."

"Try living with her."

Nate shook his head. "I like the living arrangement I've got right now, thanks."

"You're not feeling cramped in Alli's apartment?"

"We could use a little more space," his cousin admitted. "We spent a few hours on the weekend touring open houses in Westdale."

"There are some pretty big houses in that area," Ryan noted. "Are you planning on expanding your family already?"

"We're not in a hurry," Nate said. "But we both want Dylan to be settled so that if we do decide to have more kids, we won't have to uproot him again."

"What did he think of the house hunting?"

"He was right into it. At first he was just excited by the idea of having a house with an actual backyard. Then he decided it would be even better if the backyard included a pool."

Ryan chuckled at that. "So you're buying a house with a pool?"

"We put in an offer last night—we should hear back sometime today."

"There's something else on your mind," Ryan guessed.

"Yeah," Nathan admitted. "But I'm not sure if it's worth worrying you about—or even if it's anything to worry about."

"If what is?" he prompted.

"A young woman came in early this morning—I heard her talking to Alli, asking to see the CFO about some kind of scholarship program. When I walked through the door and introduced myself as the CFO, she asked specifically for John Garrett. She seemed surprised to hear that he'd retired a few months ago—and then she asked for you."

"Me?"

Nate nodded.

"Did she give you her name?"

"Nora Reardon."

"Doesn't ring any bells," Ryan told him.

"Young—probably twentysomething," Nate guessed. "Long straight dark hair, blue eyes. A little mole at the corner of her mouth."

He shook his head. "I don't think I know her."

"Okay," Nate agreed. "I just wanted to give you a heads-up in case she comes back."

"I hope she does," Ryan said. "Because now I'm curious."

"Me, too." His cousin checked his phone, grinned. "But right now I have to go buy a house."

"Congratulations."

Nate shook his hand. "Thanks."

"Just one question before you go."

He paused at the door.

"Do we have a scholarship program?"

"No," Nate told him. "We don't."

It wasn't just Oliver who was getting used to new routines. As the days turned into weeks and one month into two, she was becoming more comfortable with Ryan. She hadn't forgotten about the kiss, but she was learning to accept the way her pulse raced and her skin tingled whenever he was near.

The days leading up to Mother's Day were always chaotic as *Coffee Time with Caroline* did a full week of tributes to local mothers—including makeovers and shopping sprees and on-air cooking lessons for "In the Kitchen with Kane."

Tuesday afternoon as she pulled in the driveway, she saw a man walking toward the front door. He paused on the step when he heard her vehicle, then redirected when she got out of the car. He was young and neatly dressed in khaki pants and a collared T-shirt with some kind of logo on the chest. A salesperson, most likely.

"Harper Ross?"

The use of her name made her wary. "Yes," she acknowledged reluctantly.

He handed her an envelope. "Please read the enclosed documents carefully. You have thirty days to respond."

"Respond to what?"

"You should consult with an attorney to ensure you understand your legal options. Have a nice day, ma'am."

Then he turned on his heel and walked away.

Her fingers trembled as she lifted the flap of the envelope and pulled out a sheaf of papers. As she unfolded the crisp pages, the bold words jumped out at her.

APPLICATION FOR CUSTODY OF MINOR CHILD.

Ryan paged through the document, trying to wrap his head around the fact that Darren's sister and her husband, who'd had absolutely no contact with Oliver through the first seventeen months of his life, were suing for custody of the little boy.

He didn't think they could succeed. The possibility was, to his mind, patently ridiculous. But the fact that they'd hired an attorney and filed a petition with the court proved that they were serious, and he could tell that Harper was seriously worried.

Not three minutes earlier, she'd burst through the front door, pale and shaking and looking as if she was going to throw up. At first, he'd thought that she was actually physically ill—and then he'd seen the title of proceedings on the document that she thrust at him.

"What are we going to do?" she asked him now, her voice barely more than a whisper.

"We're going to respond," he promised her. "We're not going to let anyone take Oliver away."

Her eyes filled with tears. "I feel like this is my fault."

"How could this possibly be your fault?"

She glanced down at her white knuckles. "Because, way back in the beginning, I said that there should be someone better suited to raising Oliver than us."

He set the papers aside and reached for her hands, then unfurled her icy fingers and squeezed gently. "I guarantee you're not the only one who thought so—that doesn't make you responsible for this."

"I invited her into the house," she persisted. "I let her visit Oliver."

"Of course you did. Regardless of the fact that she lost touch with her brother a long time ago, she's still Oliver's aunt."

"We could lose Oliver," she said, her voice barely a whisper.

"We're *not* going to lose Oliver."

She didn't respond—she didn't need to. The bleak expression on her face said it all.

He shifted closer and put his arms around her. To his surprise, she leaned into him rather than pulling away, and they both drew comfort from the embrace.

"I'll call my cousin Jackson to see if he can give us a recommendation for a local attorney," he told her. "But in the meantime, there's no point in worrying about something we can't control."

"Is there something else I should worry about instead?"

His smile was wry. "I think you do enough worrying without a specific topic of concern."

"Somebody needs to."

"You think I'm not worried?"

"I don't know," she admitted. "I have no idea what goes on in your mind."

"Then I'll tell you—not a single day has gone by since Darren and Melissa died that I haven't woken up in a sweat. Every day I wonder how in hell I'm supposed to fill my best friend's shoes and worry that I can't possibly be everything that little boy wants and needs."

"You always seemed so confident and capable," she told him.

"Now you know the truth—I'm just as much in over my head as you are."

She managed a laugh. "Because there was never any doubt that I was in over my head, was there?"

"No," he admitted. "But we're making progress—all of us."

"Do you ever wonder…?"

"Do I ever wonder what?" he prompted.

"If Melissa and Darren might have made a different choice if they knew what happened between us the night of their wedding."

His brows lifted. "You mean if they knew that we'd had incredible, mind-blowing sex?"

"I'll concede to the sex," she told him. "The superlatives are editorial."

"The superlatives are just as much fact as the act."

"You're getting off topic."

"I thought the topic was the night we spent together." And thinking about that night, especially while Harper was still cuddled against his chest, was stirring not just his memories but his desires.

"No, the topic was our friends not knowing about that night," she clarified.

"You're thinking that if they did know, they wouldn't have set up this joint guardianship because they would have realized we couldn't live in close proximity and not end up in bed together again?"

"It's been a real challenge," she said drily. "But so far I've managed not to sneak naked into your bed."

"No one would blame you if, in a moment of weakness, you did," he assured her.

"I'd blame me," she told him. "Right now we need to focus on Oliver."

He rubbed her back, gently, soothingly. "I've heard that sex is an effective stress reliever."

She snorted. "I'm not *that* stressed."

But she didn't pull away from him, so he let himself hold on to her a little while longer and think about the possibilities.

Chapter Nine

As promised, Ryan called his cousin Jackson, who was a lawyer in Pinehurst, New York, and got a recommendation for a local attorney. Then he called the attorney's office and was given an appointment time of four o'clock the following afternoon.

Shelly Watts was of average height and build, but there was nothing else average about her. She had masses of wildly curling auburn hair, clear green eyes that were sharp and direct, a smile that was warm and genuine, and freckles covering every inch of visible skin.

She also had a confident manner that immediately put both of them at ease, along with a table in the corner of her office scattered with small toys, coloring books and crayons.

"I spent most of the morning in court," Shelly said after introductions had been exchanged and they were seated on the other side of her desk. "As a result, I haven't had a chance to do much more than skim the documents you dropped off, but it looks like a pretty straightforward custody dispute." She flipped through the pages of the complaint again, then set it aside. "So my question to you is—how do you want to respond?"

"Is there a way to say 'Go to hell' in legalese?" Ryan asked.

"It's instinctive to want to fight something like this," Shelly told them. "But it's not required."

"What are you saying?" Harper said.

"You're two young single people who have been entrusted with the responsibility of a minor child to whom you have no biological connection," the lawyer explained patiently. "It's not inconceivable that you might want to abdicate that responsibility to a willing party."

"We're not giving Oliver away," she said firmly.

"I'm not suggesting that you should—I just want to make sure that you're both committed to the child and the required course of action."

"We are," Ryan confirmed.

"Then let's get started."

"Do you feel better?" Ryan asked as they walked out of the lawyer's office and into the early evening.

"I'm not sure." She turned automatically toward the parking lot.

He paused on the sidewalk. "Marg & Rita's will make you feel better."

"How do you figure?"

"My cousin Tristyn says that margaritas make everything better. Plus, Marg & Rita's has decent food and I'm hungry."

"But Oliver—"

"Is with my parents," he reminded her. "And considering that they already raised three boys, I'm pretty sure they can handle one toddler for a few hours."

But he checked in with them anyway to make sure everything was okay and to ensure they didn't mind keeping Oliver a little longer. His mother was thrilled to spend more time with the little boy she'd immediately designated her first grandchild, unconcerned with the fact that he wasn't related to her by blood.

Ryan felt the same way. It didn't matter that Oliver wasn't his son—he was already looking forward to sharing all the important events in his life, from his first day of kindergarten to his first day of college. He wanted to teach him to play baseball and drive a car, to help with his math homework and commiserate with him over his first heartbreak.

He'd just hung up after talking to his mother when the waitress came to their table. Harper ordered a classic margarita and the chicken taco salad; Ryan asked for a Corona and the enchilada platter.

"This was one of Melissa's favorite restaurants," Harper told him, staring at the icy pale green liquid in her glass.

"I didn't know that," he admitted.

She nodded. "Darren did—he brought her here for dinner the night he proposed."

"I thought he proposed in the movie theater."

"He did. But they came here first. He'd planned to give her the ring at dinner, but he chickened out because the restaurant was crowded and he didn't want too many witnesses if she said no to his proposal. So he waited until they were inside the darkened movie theater and put the ring in the popcorn box instead."

She smiled a little at the memory. "Melissa always liked to joke about his 'corny' proposal, but I know she thought it was incredibly romantic."

"It wouldn't have been nearly as romantic if the ring

had slipped to the bottom of the box and she'd thrown it into the garbage," he noted.

"I don't think he would have let that happen."

"He was so nervous," Ryan remembered. "I thought it was because he was the first of our group of college friends to take such a big step, but he said it was because she was such an integral part of his life and his heart, he couldn't imagine a single day of his life without her."

"He said that?"

"Sappy, huh?"

"It's not sappy," she denied. "It's perfect."

"Darren always was a romantic."

She nodded. "And every year, on the anniversary of his proposal, he took Melissa back to the same movie theater."

"I didn't know that part," Ryan admitted. "But it's precisely that kind of thing that makes the rest of us look bad. It's hard enough for a guy to remember birthdays and real anniversaries, but to remember the anniversary of the date that he proposed?"

"He also sent her flowers every year on the anniversary of the day they met," she told him.

He shook his head in mock disapproval. "That kind of thing, too."

"He loved her," she said simply.

"He did," Ryan confirmed, his tone serious now. "He fell for her hard and fast and never looked back."

"They were good together," Harper agreed. "I know they sometimes argued—and sometimes about stupid things— but there was never any doubt about their commitment to one another."

"Why does that make you sad?" he asked, because he could tell by the emotions swirling in the depths of her chocolate-colored eyes and the wistful tone of her voice that it did.

"Talking about them in the past tense—it just feels so wrong. And it breaks my heart to realize that Oliver won't have any real memories of how much his parents loved one another—and him."

"He might not remember, but he'll know," Ryan said. "We'll make sure that he knows."

"Unless—"

He reached across the table to cover her hand with his own. "No one is going to take Oliver away from us."

It wasn't really a promise he could make, but she nodded, apparently reassured. Or at least pretending to be.

On Sunday morning, Harper got up early with the intention of being showered and dressed and ready to go before Oliver woke up. Ryan had invited her to brunch at his parents' house—a Mother's Day tradition in his family—but there was somewhere else she wanted to go first.

Of course, she should have known that Oliver wouldn't cooperate with her plan, and when she went to get him up, she found that he was already awake—and so was Ryan.

"What are you doing up?" he asked. "I thought you'd take advantage of the opportunity to sleep in this morning."

She shook her head. "Since you're going to brunch at your parents' house—"

"*We're* going to brunch," he interjected.

"Since *we're* going to brunch at your parents' house, I wanted to take Oliver for a short drive this morning."

"Anywhere in particular?"

She could tell by the tone of his question that he already suspected her destination, so she nodded. "The cemetery."

Oliver was obviously too young to understand the significance of the day, but she felt it was important to take some time to recognize the woman who had brought him into the world.

Ryan nodded, somehow instinctively understanding everything she couldn't say. "Give me fifteen minutes to shower, and I'll go with you."

"You don't have to," she hastened to assure him.

His brows lifted. "Is there a reason you don't want me to go with you?"

"Maybe I don't want you to see me cry."

"I've seen you cry before," he reminded her.

She didn't need him to remind her of the meltdown she'd had at the hospital—or the kiss that had followed. She'd spent far too much time thinking of the two kisses they'd shared in recent weeks, pondering Ryan's insistence that the next move had to be hers and wondering if she'd ever have the courage to make that move—or even admit that she wanted to.

But the only move she was going to make this morning was out the door.

"Then we should get moving to make sure we're not late for brunch."

Harper was quiet throughout the drive, thinking about Melissa and wishing her friend could be here to celebrate this special day with her son. Melissa had loved Oliver so much, and it wasn't just tragic but unfair that she'd been taken from his life so early.

"They say that as children grow, they lose the ability to retain any real memories of events that occurred prior to their third or fourth birthdays," she said when Ryan pulled into the parking lot of Woodhaven Cemetery.

"Who says?"

"Most of the books I've been reading."

"And you're worried that Oliver won't remember his parents," he guessed.

She nodded. "We can talk about them and show him pictures, but there's going to come a time when his memories will fade away." She looked at the little boy in the back, playing with his beanbag puppy, and sighed. "Maybe they already have."

"We can't do anything about that," Ryan said gently. "All we can do is give him the love and support that Melissa and Darren would have."

She nodded. "And we will."

"Up!" Oliver demanded when Ryan opened the back door to let him out of the car.

"Up," he confirmed, lifting the baby into his arms.

"Woof!" The little boy held up his puppy.

"Woof! Woof!" Ryan said, making him giggle.

They walked side by side between the rows of markers. Ryan carried the baby on his left hip; Harper carried the bouquet of flowers in her right hand, her other linked with his. They might have different opinions and ideas about a lot of things, but in their commitment to honor their friends' wishes, they were united, and she was glad he'd offered to come with her today.

The sun was high, the sky clear and blue, the grass lush and green. It was a picture-perfect day.

"It rained last Mother's Day," Harper told Ryan.

"How is it that you remember that?"

"Because Melissa told me that Darren had planned to celebrate the occasion with a picnic in the park, but it was too wet. Instead he pushed back the furniture and set up their picnic in the middle of the living room."

"That sounds like something he would do."

"They ate sandwiches off paper plates and drank wine out of plastic cups, and she loved every minute of it."

And then Darren had shoved the picnic basket aside, laid his wife down on the blanket and made love to her—which was something they wouldn't have been able to do in the park. So maybe the rain was a blessing after all, Melissa had confided. Of course, Harper didn't share that part of her memory with Ryan.

It broke Harper's heart to realize that Melissa's first Mother's Day with her son was also the last that she would ever celebrate. And while Harper would always regret that her friend's life had been tragically cut short, she found some comfort in knowing that every day Melissa had been alive, she had lived.

Her friend had always urged Harper to do the same—to step outside her comfort zone and try new things. Seize the day, she'd advised, because you couldn't ever know what tomorrow would bring.

When they arrived at the polished granite stone etched with their friends' names, Harper noticed that the vase beside the marker was already filled with fresh flowers.

She looked at Ryan; he shrugged.

"I was ordering other flowers yesterday and I thought Oliver would like to get some for his mom."

She realized that she wasn't really surprised. Over the past few weeks, he'd demonstrated his thoughtfulness and kindness in countless ways—this was only the latest example. And only one of the reasons she was fighting a losing battle against her growing feelings for him.

Oliver dropped his puppy, so Ryan set him on his feet to retrieve it. He picked up the toy, then moved to the flowers by his mother's grave and patted the colorful blossoms. "Pi-ty."

"They're very pretty," Harper agreed. "We've got some more pretty flowers for Mommy, too."

"Ma-ma," he echoed.

She nodded, her throat tight, and took the little boy's hand so that he could help her put the flowers in the vase on the other side of the marker.

"I bet Darren would rather have a beer than a bouquet," Ryan commented, making her smile through her tears.

"We'll have to keep that in mind for Father's Day," she said.

They stood quietly for a few minutes, both lost in their own thoughts, while Oliver sat in the grass and played with Woof. When they were ready to go, Harper lifted him into her arms.

"Can you blow kisses for Mommy?" she asked, demonstrating with her own hand how it was done.

Oliver mimicked her, putting his open hand to his mouth and making a smacking noise.

"Just like that," she confirmed.

Then he leaned forward and planted his lips on hers.

Twenty minutes later, Ryan pulled into the wide driveway in front of his parents' sprawling bungalow. He parked behind Justin's sporty new BMW, but he didn't see any sign of Braden's Mercedes sedan.

Ellen greeted all of them with hugs and kisses and immediately stole Oliver from his arms.

"I was afraid we'd be the last ones here," Ryan said.

"You are," his mother said.

"Braden and Dana aren't coming?"

She shook her head.

"Dana has decided that Mother's Day is a personal affront to all childless women." Justin was standing at the stove, pushing fried potatoes around in a pan, his tone clearly expressing displeasure with his sister-in-law.

"Justin," Ellen chided.

"Braden and Dana have been trying—unsuccessfully—

to have a baby for a couple of years," Ryan explained to Harper.

"More like four years," Ellen said. "They wanted to keep it quiet at first, waiting to share the big news when it finally happened—but it hasn't happened."

"That must be heartbreaking for both of them."

Ellen nodded. "Of course, when they told me they wanted to have a baby, I was so thrilled about the prospect of becoming a grandmother I might have made too much of a big deal about it. And I worry now that I might have put more pressure on my daughter-in-law."

"I could have stayed home with Oliver," Harper said. "If the baby's presence would make her uncomfortable."

"You could not have stayed home," Ellen denied. "I wouldn't have allowed it. In fact, I was hoping that seeing you and Ryan with Oliver would show Dana and Braden that family is about more than biology."

"I feel like I'm missing something," Harper admitted.

"After six months of fertility treatments without a pregnancy, Braden suggested that they should look into adoption," Ellen explained. "Dana nixed that idea."

"Why?"

His mother shrugged. "Near as I can tell, she doesn't want someone else's baby."

Harper frowned at that but said nothing. Not really knowing Braden or Dana, she was probably reluctant to comment, but he suspected she felt as he did—that a woman who apparently desperately wanted a baby wouldn't turn away from any child who needed a family.

"But that's enough about that," Ellen said. "Today I want to celebrate my first Mother's Day as a grandma."

They did so by indulging in a meal that included thick slices of French toast, fluffy scrambled eggs, spicy fried potatoes, crisp maple bacon, fresh fruit and mimosas—all prepared by Ellen's husband and children. At least, that had been the tradition since the kids had been small, but the reality was that John did most of the cooking now and their sons showed up when it was ready to go on the table.

After brunch they had coffee in the back garden. By then it was getting close to Oliver's usual nap time and—proof that he was starting to feel sleepy—he asked for Woof. Harper looked through every pocket and compartment of the diaper bag with no success. "Did he leave it in the car?" she wondered.

"Woof?" Ellen queried.

"His beanbag puppy."

"I'll check the car," Ryan said. "I know he had it when we left the house."

"He had it at the cemetery, too."

Ellen cuddled the boy on her lap while they went to look for the toy.

Ryan checked the back, even behind Oliver's car seat and under the floor mats, while Harper checked the front. They both came up empty-handed.

"Do you think he left it at the cemetery?"

Harper sighed. "I honestly don't know where else it could be."

"I'll go back," he decided.

"I feel like I should tell you that you don't have to, but…"

"But it's his favorite toy," Ryan finished for her.

She nodded.

"I'll be back in about half an hour."

While Ryan was gone, Harper lingered over a second cup of coffee with Ellen while the other men cleaned up the dishes. Justin grumbled that Ryan had probably hidden Oliver's toy just to skip out on doing his part, but he refused Harper's offers to help, insisting that "Mother's Day Rules" meant no one with two X chromosomes was allowed to cook or clean.

Harper sipped her coffee. "I think I could learn to like those rules."

Ellen smiled. "It's fun to be spoiled by my men every once in a while," she agreed. "Of course, for the next week I'll be cursing them every time I can't find a bowl or a spoon because nothing gets put back in the right place."

Harper chuckled softly.

Ellen looked down at the little boy snuggled against her chest, his thumb in his mouth, his eyes closed. "It seems like forever since my boys were this small."

"And he already seems so much bigger than he was two months ago."

"They grow fast," Ellen agreed, gently rubbing the baby's back. "So what are your plans for the rest of the day?"

"To do as little as possible," Harper confided.

"You won't be visiting your family later?"

She shook her head. "They're all in New York City."

"I visited Manhattan once. It was…" Ellen paused, searching for an appropriate description. "…big. And busy."

"It is both," she agreed.

"Do you get back to New York often?"

"A couple of times a year."

"How did you end up in Charisma?"

"I was offered a job at WNCC." She sipped her coffee. "Actually, I also had job offers in Rock Springs, Wyoming, and Ankeny, Iowa—I chose Charisma because Melissa was coming back here."

"How long have you been at WNCC?"

"Almost five years. The last three with *Coffee Time*."

"Is it exciting—working in television?"

"It's exhausting," Harper admitted.

"But you enjoy it?"

"I wouldn't still be doing it if I didn't."

"I watch your show every morning," Ellen said. "It's very entertaining."

"Caroline is a fabulous host," Harper agreed.

"But what is she *really* like? Is she a taskmaster or a diva? I promise—anything you tell me won't go any further."

"She's a consummate professional who demands the best from her staff and herself. She's also an incredibly sweet and warm person."

"Really?" Ryan's mom sounded a little disappointed.

"Really," Harper assured her.

"What about Kane?"

She smiled. "Women always want to know about Kane—but they never want to hear the truth."

"What's the truth?"

"That he *is* a diva."

Ellen laughed. "You must meet so many interesting people in your line of work."

"I do," she agreed.

"I worked at a lot of different jobs over the years, some I liked more than others, but none ever meant more to me than being a mother."

"It shows," Harper said sincerely.

"It wasn't always easy—in fact, it usually wasn't easy at all. But when I look at my three grown sons, I can't help but feel proud of them and pleased that I was able to play a small part in helping them become the men that they are."

"But she's most proud of me," Justin said as he came back out onto the deck.

Ellen smiled indulgently. "Of course, any mother would be thrilled to have a son who is a doctor."

"See?" he said, winking at Harper.

"The title proves that you're smart, driven and successful," Ellen noted. "But it doesn't mean you're not lonely."

"I'm not lonely," he assured her.

"Sometimes a man doesn't realize how much he wants a partner to share his life until he finds the right partner."

"I like my life exactly as it is."

"Right now there's no reason you shouldn't," his mother agreed.

"And right now I have to go—I'm on the afternoon shift today."

He bent down to kiss his mother's cheek, then surprised Harper by kissing hers, too. "Happy Mother's Day."

Chapter Ten

Despite his promise to return in thirty minutes, it was nearly twice that amount of time before Ryan came back. And he came back empty-handed.

"I traced our route twice," he told Harper. "I even went back to the house and double-checked, just in case we were wrong about him having it earlier."

"What are we going to do?"

Ryan shrugged. "I have no idea."

"You might want to stop by the Toy Depot on the way home to see if they have anything similar," Ellen suggested. "Even if they don't, he could pick out a new toy that might help him forget about Woof, at least for a few days."

"Do you think that will work?" Harper asked.

"Ryan had a favorite blanket when he was a baby— until he was six years old. He took it everywhere with him, which meant it had to go through the washing machine more times than I could count, until one day it finally fell apart. I bought at least half a dozen blankets trying to replace it, and each new one seemed to make him happy the first time he went to sleep with it—and the next day, he'd scream for blankie again."

Harper looked at Ryan, her lips twitching. "Blankie?"

"I think she's making it up."

"I am not making it up," his mother said primly.

"Then maybe you're mistaken—maybe it was Braden who had the blankie."

"It was you," she insisted. "I'm not making it up and I'm not mistaken, because I ended up sewing a ragged scrap from the original blanket to the ear of your teddy bear so that you could hold on to that while you fell asleep."

"Did that work?" Harper asked.

"He slept with that bear until he was twelve."

"And on that note," Ryan said, picking up Oliver's diaper bag, "I think it's time for us to go."

"I'm not in a hurry," Harper said with a devilish smile. "And I'll bet your mom has a lot more stories to tell."

Ellen chuckled. "Days'—maybe weeks'—worth of stories."

"Unfortunately, the Toy Depot is only open until five," Ryan said.

"Then you better get going," his mother agreed.

When they got home from the toy store with a stuffed Dalmatian that didn't really look anything like Woof except that it was a dog, Harper discovered an enormous bouquet of flowers on the coffee table in the living room.

"Pi-ty," Oliver said, pointing to the flowers.

Harper nodded as she picked up the card, her eyes blurring with tears as she read the childlike printing.

For my new mommy on her first Mother's Day. Love, Oliver. xoxo.

She looked from the message to Ryan. "Crayon?"

"He doesn't yet have the dexterity to hold a pen," he explained.

"If you really wanted me to believe that Oliver wrote the card, you should have spelled one or two words incorrectly."

"Okay—I helped with the front. But he wrote on the back."

She turned the card over to discover there was a blue scribble on the reverse side. "That does look slightly more age appropriate," she agreed.

"Since you've been reading that book, you think you're an expert on everything, don't you?" Ryan teased.

"Even before I read that book, I wouldn't have believed that a child could correctly print words he isn't even able to pronounce clearly." She picked up the little boy and gave him a smacking kiss on the cheek. "Thank you for the pretty flowers, Oliver."

"Pi-ty," he said again.

"If you don't believe he wrote the card, you probably don't believe he drove himself to the flower shop," Ryan said. "So shouldn't I get a thank-you, too?"

"Thank you," she said.

His brows lifted. "What about a kiss for me?"

She took a step closer and let her gaze settle on his lips.

Then she chickened out and kissed his cheek. He looked disappointed but not really surprised.

They spent a quiet evening together. Ryan and Oliver played with his blocks while Harper divided her attention between the pages of *What to Expect* and the movie *27 Dresses* on television, not able to focus on either, because she was thinking about Melissa. Not her tragic death but her philosophy for life: *carpe diem.*

"You've been quiet since we got back," Ryan commented later, after Oliver was settled into bed. "Are you still thinking about Melissa?"

She nodded, wishing that she could be fearless like her friend and reach out for what she wanted.

And why couldn't she?

Ryan had told her that the next move was hers—why shouldn't she make it?

She rose up on her toes to brush her lips against his. "This is my move."

Then she took his hand and led him into her bedroom.

He followed willingly. Even eagerly. And his eyes darkened with unmistakable desire when she tugged his shirt out of his pants and slid her hands beneath it.

His lips skimmed down the column of her throat, making electricity hum just beneath the surface of her skin, currents that zipped through her blood and arrowed straight to her core. She'd told him over and over again that she didn't want this—had told herself the same thing. But her response to his lightest touch proved to both of them that she was a liar.

He nibbled on her earlobe, then sucked it gently into his mouth, and her knees actually trembled.

"Ryan…"

"If you've changed your mind and decided you don't want this, say it now, Harper—loud and clear—before we go any further."

But it had already gone further. His hand had found its way to her breast, and though he was stroking his thumb over the peaked nipple through the multiple layers of her blouse, camisole and bra, she felt scorched by his touch, as if there was no barrier between his hand and her flesh.

His mouth skimmed across her jaw. "Yes or no?"

Her breath shuddered out. "Yes."

She felt the curve of his lips as his mouth continued to tease her with soft, fleeting kisses. "Yes—what?"

"Yes, I want you."

He traced the outline of her lips with his tongue. "There will be no walking away in the morning," he warned her. "Not this time."

"I know."

"It's going to get messy."

"I hope so."

He chuckled against her lips. "Emotionally, too."

She wasn't quite on board with that. "We're friends now—and we both love Oliver, so we'll figure it out."

"We're friends," he confirmed. "And we're going to be lovers."

"Then maybe you should stop talking and start doing."

"Doing what?" He'd already unbuttoned her blouse and pushed it off her shoulders now. "What is it, exactly, that you want me to do?"

She felt the heat fill her cheeks. "To stop talking."

He lifted the camisole over her head, discarded it, then reached for the fastening of the bra at her back but paused. "I want to know what you want, what you like."

"I'm sure you can figure it out."

He was sure that he could, too. But he wasn't going to make it easy this time—for either of them.

He needed to hear her say that she wanted him—he needed to know that her desire was at least half of his own. He needed to know that he could control her body, because when he was with her, he no longer controlled his own. When he was with her, he could think of nothing but her, want no one but her.

The wanting didn't bother him—it was the intensity of it, the urgency and desperation. Never had he wanted a woman so much; never had want come so perilously close to need.

Making her lose control allowed him to feel as if he had a little of his own back.

His fingers skimmed up her back to the tops of her shoulders, hooked in the straps of her bra and tugged them down her arms. Then he lowered his head and kissed the tops of her breasts, his lips brushing over them in a teasing caress that promised more. So much more.

"Tell me," he said again.

"That," she admitted. "I love when you do that."

"Kiss your breasts?"

She nodded.

"Say it, Harper." He nudged the lacy cups of her bra down a little farther, exposing more creamy skin.

"I love when you kiss my breasts."

His lips brushed over the curves again, dipping toward the edge of her areola, then withdrawing again. He felt the tension in her, knew what she wanted, what she didn't want to ask for. "Just like that?" he asked. "Is that what you meant? Or do you like when I lick—" his tongue flicked over one peak "—and suck—" he shifted his attention and pulled the other one deep into his mouth "—your nipples?"

She moaned softly.

"Tell me," he demanded.

"I like—oh…I like…that."

She was aroused. He could hear it in the tempo of her breathing, see it in the way her breasts rose and fell with each shallow breath. He could feel it in the thunderous pounding of her heart beneath his lips, a frantic rhythm that matched his own.

He unclasped her bra now, fully releasing her breasts from the lacy cups. She gasped as the cool air hit her skin, as her already-peaked nipples tightened further.

She was so incredibly beautiful. And nervous. He wasn't sure how he knew it, but he didn't doubt that it was true.

He swirled his tongue around one of the rosy peaks, then the other.

She gasped again. "Yes," she told him. "Like that."

He drew the nipple into his mouth, tugging gently on it with his teeth, and she arched beneath him. "And that?"

"Yes," she agreed breathlessly.

He continued to tease the aroused flesh with his lips and his tongue while he worked her skirt over her hips. The lacy bikini panties she wore matched the already-discarded bra, so he sent them in the same direction. Then she was completely naked beneath him, bared to his gaze. Her skin was soft and fragrant, so sweetly and tantalizingly feminine.

He lifted his mouth from her breast, blew softly on the wet tip. She moaned softly. "Ryan."

"Tell me what you want," he reminded her.

"You," she said. "I want you."

His lips moved down her body, kissing and nibbling the warm, silky flesh. She was passionate and responsive, and when she wrapped herself around him, she felt darn close to perfect.

The one night they'd spent together continued to haunt him. They'd both been a little drunk and desperately eager as they finally succumbed to the attraction that had been simmering between them for more than two years already, and as spectacular as it had been in his memory, he'd started to wonder if it had been less so for her.

He wasn't at all drunk tonight, and he was determined to ensure that this experience wasn't just memorable but truly unforgettable. He spread her legs wide and lowered his head between them. He heard her breath catch in her throat, felt the tension in the muscles of her thighs beneath his hands.

"Do you like that?"

"You can't tell?"

"I want to hear you say it."

"I like when you touch me there…kiss me there."

He suspected it would push her way beyond her comfort zone to ask her to clarify "there." Instead he said, "Tell me you want more."

She sighed. "I want…more."

So he gave her more.

And he took more.

He nibbled and licked and savored. He made her back arch and her breath catch and her body collapse. And then he drove her up again, taking her to the pinnacle of pleasure, letting her hover there while he protected both of them and finally buried himself in the wet haven between her thighs.

Harper rose up to wrap herself around him, her fingernails digging into his shoulders, her ankles locking around his waist. They'd both wanted, and fought against, exactly this—for too long. Now they were united in their desire and their purpose, and she met him thrust for thrust in a fast and frantic race to the finish.

"I thought maybe I'd fooled myself into thinking that the lovemaking we shared the night of Melissa and Darren's wedding was more spectacular than it was," Harper admitted to him later, when they were both sprawled naked and exhausted across her bed. "I was wrong."

"Told you," Ryan said, just a little smugly.

"That night was the most incredible experience of my life."

"Until tonight, you mean."

She smiled. "Until tonight."

"So why did you say that first night was a mistake?" he asked her.

"Because I was afraid that you would think it was."

"I don't think I said or did anything to give you that impression."

"You didn't," she agreed. "But I didn't have—still don't have—a lot of experience with relationships. And my parents' on-again, off-again marriage wasn't any kind of example. And when I woke up the next morning, I didn't know what to expect from you—or what you expected from me."

"You said it was a mistake anticipating that I might think it was?"

She nodded. "Melissa always accused me of sabotaging my own relationships to ensure that I had control over when they ended. Because the only thing I was ever sure of was that they would end.

"That's one of the reasons this is so scary to me," she admitted. "Because no matter what happens between us, our connection to Oliver means that neither of us can walk away."

"I don't want to walk away," he told her.

"Not right at this minute," she allowed.

"Because I'm exactly where I want to be."

"Naked in my bed?"

"With you," he clarified.

Harper woke up in the middle of the night and found herself alone.

More surprising than that fact was the realization she was disappointed to be alone, that she wanted Ryan to be with her still.

She wondered where he'd gone—and why. Had she scared him off with her talk about relationships? Had she assumed too much?

She'd seized the day—but not without some trepidation. Making love with Ryan had been a big step for her, and she knew it wasn't just possible but likely that he would break her heart. Because, the example of his family aside, Harper knew better than to believe in happy endings.

But she wasn't going to worry about the future, what might or might not happen between them. She was only going to enjoy being with him now. Or she would, except for the fact that the bed beside her was empty.

And then she saw him in the doorway. He stood there for a moment, as if undecided whether or not to cross the threshold, whether to stay or go.

She held her breath, waiting.

He stepped into the room.

"Is Oliver okay?" she asked quietly.

"Yeah. He was fussing a little, but he settled right down again." He sat on the edge of the mattress. "Are *you* okay?"

She shouldn't have been surprised that he would ask, that he would worry. Over the past two months, they'd spent a lot of time together and got to know one another better. She might even go so far as to say that they'd become friends, and she didn't doubt that he cared about her the same way she cared about him.

"Actually," she finally said in response to his question, "I was just thinking that it's a little chilly in here."

"Do you want me to turn off the AC?"

"No, I want you to slide under the covers and warm me up."

His lips curved into that slow sexy smile that never failed to make her heart sigh. "That I can do."

And then his lips were on hers, his hands were stroking over her body, and she sighed in blissful pleasure.

"I was a little worried that it might be awkward," he admitted to her now.

"The act or afterward?"

"Afterward."

"Why did you think it might be?"

"Because we've been here before," he reminded her.

"Everything was different then."

"How do you figure?"

"Four years ago, I didn't know you very well, and what I did know about you, I wasn't sure I liked."

He quirked a brow. "So how did we end up in bed together?"

"I blame the champagne," she told him. "That—and your very hot body."

"I never would have guessed that you were so shallow," he said, but he sounded more amused than offended.

"Apparently I am. Or was."

"You don't think my body's so hot anymore?"

"I know there's more to you than a hot body now."

"You do, huh?"

She nodded as she slid her palms up his torso, gliding over the ridges of his abdomen, caressing the smooth pectorals. "I know you're not just educated but smart—smarter than most people realize." Smarter than she'd realized, until recently. "That you're not just strong but gentle." And she'd had no idea how appealing that combination could be. "You're also warm and funny and kind and caring."

"Apparently I'm quite a catch," he mused.

"As if you'd ever let yourself be caught."

"I might," he told her. "By the right woman."

"Really?"

"You sound surprised."

She shrugged. "Maybe because you always gave the impression that you were looking for a good time, not a long time."

"I probably was," he acknowledged.

"What changed?"

"Oliver." He smiled. "Who would have figured that I'd

be the first of my brothers to have a child—or at least the responsibility for one?"

"Darren obviously had faith that you were up to the challenge."

"I've always liked kids," he admitted. "They just weren't anywhere on my radar until Oliver landed in my lap."

"Not mine, either."

"And yet we're doing pretty good as a family."

"Do you really think so?"

"Do you doubt it?"

"Some days," she admitted.

"Why?"

"I guess because I'm not really sure what a family should be. I know my own isn't ideal. Not even close."

"And you think mine is?"

"Maybe not ideal," she acknowledged. But she'd spent enough time with them to see that they were committed not just to the idea of family but to one another. When any of them needed anything, the relatives descended en masse to help out. As was evidenced by the freezer still full of casseroles and an extensive waiting list of aunts and cousins who wanted to babysit Oliver. "But they're wonderful."

"They think you're pretty wonderful, too—although my mother worries that you're a little on the skinny side."

"Skinny?"

He nodded.

"What do you think?"

"You're soft and warm and naked, which makes you just about perfect in my book."

Chapter Eleven

As soon as she stepped through the door, Harper was greeted by a series of high, sharp barks—the universal language of puppies—accompanied by the scrabble of little nails racing across the ceramic tile.

Oliver was right on the heels of the canine, jumping up and down and saying, "Woof. Woof. Woof."

The furry bundle skidded to a sliding stop at her feet and looked up at her with big brown eyes that would melt a colder heart than hers. But she didn't pick it up—or even reach down to pat the silky little head. She kept her fingers wrapped firmly around the strap of her briefcase and looked at Ryan, who had followed the puppy and toddler into the room, and said, "No."

He offered her a sheepish grin. "It's not what you think."

"There isn't a puppy at my feet?"

"Woof. Woof. Woof," Oliver said again.

"Two puppies," she amended.

"The furry one belongs to Braden," Ryan told her.

She exhaled a little at that. "Okay, but that still doesn't explain why she's here instead of at your brother's house," she said, assuming on the basis of the pink collar studded with rhinestones that the puppy was female.

"She's an anniversary present for Dana, but their anniversary isn't until the end of next week, so Braden asked if we could keep her until then. I know I should have checked with you first," he hastened to say. "But...well, Coco looked at me with those eyes, and I just couldn't say no."

"Cocoa? It's apt, if not very original."

"Not C-O-C-O-A but C-O-C-O," he explained. "Like the designer."

"That's a little more original," she agreed. "But if their anniversary isn't until the end of next week, why didn't Braden wait until then to get a puppy?"

"Because he saw the puppies on the SPCA website and he knew they'd all be gone before then."

Of course they would, because if the others looked anything like Coco, they were too adorable for words. But having a puppy in the house, even for a short time, made her uneasy. "I'm not sure this is a good idea."

"Woof," Oliver said again, crouching down and gently patting the puppy's head.

"He does look like Woof," she said to Ryan. "And you know how devastated he was when he lost that toy—what's going to happen when your brother takes Coco away?"

He'd apparently already thought that one out. "He'll be fine, because we can go to Braden and Dana's house to visit Coco."

Harper wasn't convinced.

"Or we could go to the SPCA to get one of Coco's brothers or sisters for Oliver."

"No," she said quickly. Definitively. "It's bad enough that a puppy needs so much time and attention, but then it grows up to be a dog."

"You don't like dogs?"

"I don't dislike dogs," she said cautiously.

"You never had a pet?" he guessed.

"I had a hamster, when I was eleven."

Ryan scooped Coco up off the floor and held the puppy out to her.

She folded her arms over her chest; he chuckled.

"What are you afraid of?"

"I'm afraid she's going to piddle on the hardwood floors or chew my favorite designer shoes."

He shook his head. "You're afraid of falling in love."

She rolled her eyes.

Oliver reached up to pat the puppy's head; Coco swiped at his chin with her tongue; the little boy giggled; and Harper felt something inside her heart just melt.

"I don't know the first thing about dogs," she told him, determined to establish the parameters of her relationship with the canine. "So I'm not looking after it when you go to work this afternoon."

Anticipating just such a response, Ryan had wisely booked the day off, and after lunch he persuaded Harper to accompany them to the park.

There was a matching pink leash to go with the collar but Ryan didn't dare ask Harper to hold it while they walked. She'd made it more than clear that the puppy was his responsibility—at least until Braden picked him up.

They weren't halfway to the park when he noticed that Coco was having trouble keeping up. Though her tail was still wagging, her little legs simply couldn't match their pace, so he picked her up and put her in the basket beneath Oliver's seat. Coco promptly curled into a ball and fell asleep.

By the time they arrived at their destination, Coco proved that she'd been rejuvenated by her short nap, racing in circles around the climber while Oliver played on it.

Although Harper tried to hold herself aloof, several times Ryan caught her laughing at the puppy's antics. He loved to hear her laugh, and neither of them had had much reason to laugh over the past couple of months. When it was time to make the return trip home, she took Coco's leash, and when the puppy began to fall behind again, she picked her up and carried her.

He kept a close eye on Coco throughout the rest of the day. Although it seemed apparent that Harper had fallen for the puppy as quickly as he had, he'd promised that he wouldn't let Coco roam freely through the house so they wouldn't have to worry about little puddles on the floor or presents behind the furniture. He had caught the puppy starting to squat in the house a couple of times, but he'd managed to get her outside before she actually piddled. But at some point, while he'd been at the computer, Coco had got up from her bed beside the desk and wandered off— and he had no idea where.

He poked his head into the family room, where Harper had set herself up with her tablet after Oliver had gone to bed. The TV was now on, the tablet had been set aside, and Coco was in her lap.

"She's only going to be here for about a week," he reminded Harper.

The hand that was absently stroking the soft fur behind the puppy's ears stilled. "I see you finally realized she was missing."

"She hasn't been gone that long," he said, though he really wasn't sure.

"Almost an hour," she told him, resuming her stroking.

He sat on the arm of the sofa and scratched the puppy under her chin. Coco sighed.

"Whatever made your brother think to get his wife a puppy as an anniversary present?" she asked curiously.

"I think Braden's grasping at straws, desperately trying to make her happy."

"It must be hard for her," she said. "To be surrounded by people with babies and not be able to have one herself."

"There are other options for a woman who really wants a child," he pointed out. "And a lot of kids in this world in need of a family."

"Why aren't they considering adoption?"

"Because adoption is a viable option."

"I don't understand."

"Claiming to want a baby but not being able to have one keeps the focus on Dana. If they adopted, the attention would shift to the baby."

"That's harsh," Harper chided, continuing to stroke the puppy's back.

"It is," he agreed. "But not inaccurate."

"Since I've never met your sister-in-law, I'm hardly in a position to argue," she admitted.

"And if you had met her, you wouldn't."

"But speaking of women I have met—was Aubrey here today?"

"No," he told her, wondering at the odd segue to that question.

"I thought I saw her this afternoon," Harper said. "But I'm sure if she'd been in town, she would have wanted to see Oliver."

Ryan frowned. "Where did you think you saw her?"

"When I was leaving the studio. I glanced across the street and she was there, looking in the window of the bookstore. I only caught a quick glimpse, and when I looked back again, she was gone."

"So you're not sure it was her?"

"No," she admitted, but he could tell by the tone of her voice that she felt uneasy. "Like I said, it was a quick glimpse and then she was gone."

"They say everyone has a twin somewhere," he reminded her.

"It just seems too much of a coincidence—a woman who looks like Aubrey hovering in the area where I work." She shook her head. "Or maybe I'm just paranoid. Because if it was Aubrey—why wouldn't she stop by to see Oliver?"

"That's a good question," he agreed.

"So the answer is most likely that the woman I saw wasn't Aubrey at all," she decided.

He hoped she was right.

As Aubrey drove back to Martinsville, she was already thinking about everything she wanted to do to get the house ready for Oliver's arrival.

Early in their marriage, she and Jeremy planned to fill their house with children. Two miscarriages in the first three years of their marriage had proved that it wouldn't be easy, but neither of them had given up. For the next year, Jeremy had been diligent about birth control until the doctor said it was safe to try again. Two months later, she was pregnant.

When she made it to week sixteen, she and Jeremy had a quiet celebration. At week twenty, they started talking about decorating a room for their baby. In week twenty-four, they ordered the crib and change table. She marveled at the changes to her body, relished every movement of the baby in her womb. Week twenty-six, they painted. Week twenty-eight, the baby stopped moving.

She didn't tell anyone. She refused to believe that God could be so cruel as to take another child from her. At her thirty-week checkup, the doctor couldn't detect a heartbeat. He sent her to the hospital, where they took the dead baby girl from her womb. They named their daughter Angel and buried her beside Jeremy's mother at Holy Cross Cemetery.

Jeremy moved the crib and change table into the attic and painted over the pale yellow walls of the nursery, turning it into a home office. She cried and pleaded with him not to give up, but he said that he couldn't stand to watch her heart break over and over again.

She knew he grieved for their lost babies, too, but it was different for him. He had four children from his first marriage. In fact, by that time, his eldest son was about to have a child of his own—Jeremy was going to be a grandfather, and she had never experienced the joy of holding her own child in her arms.

But now it was finally going to happen.

Jeremy had warned her not to get her hopes up when she told him she wanted to raise her brother's child. As an attorney, he knew to expect the unexpected in court. But she was confident that when the judge finally heard their case, he would decide that she and Jeremy could provide a better home for Oliver than his appointed guardians could.

And she was determined to have everything ready for him when that happened. When they finally got to bring him home, she wanted him to know that he would be there to stay—with his family, where he belonged.

Harper's invitation for Aubrey to visit Oliver anytime she wanted had been sincere. She wanted the little boy to have a relationship with his father's sister and her husband, but the whole being-sued-for-custody thing had made her less inclined to welcome the other couple into their home.

Of course, now that Aubrey and Jeremy had instigated legal action, she didn't really have a choice. Shelly had told them that they had to play nice with Oliver's aunt and uncle, which meant allowing them to visit and establish a relationship with the child. And even that might not have been so bad if they hadn't stopped by the previous weekend when Oliver's litigation guardian happened to be there at the same time.

Harper had been surprised to discover how much of an age difference there was between Aubrey and Jeremy—at least twenty years, she guessed, and understood why that had been an issue for Aubrey's parents when she was only eighteen. But there was no disputing that he was good with Oliver—or that he was going along with the custody application because it was what Aubrey wanted.

He explained to the litigation guardian that his busy criminal law practice required that his wife would be the primary caregiver if their application for custody was successful. And although Aubrey currently worked—primarily with the infants in a local day care in Martinsville—she would happily give up her job to be a full-time caregiver to their nephew.

After that visit, Harper wasn't nearly as confident that a judge would rule in favor of the status quo.

And when the bell rang the following Saturday morning—followed by Coco's incessant barking to ensure she was aware that someone was at the door—Harper was understandably cautious. She peeked through the living room window before responding to the summons. Pleasure overcame wariness when she recognized the woman and little boy at the door.

"Ohmygod," Kenna said when Harper opened the door with Oliver by her side and Coco in her arms. "You got a puppy."

"No," she said quickly. "We're just puppy-sitting for a short while."

"Oh, but she's so cute."

"Cute and loud and demanding," Harper said. "Kind of like having a second child."

Kenna chuckled and hitched Jacob a little higher on her hip. "Do you want a third?"

"Not forever, but you're welcome to come in for a visit."

"We're just out dropping off invitations for Jacob's first birthday party," Kenna told her, prompting the baby to give Harper the envelope in his hand.

"That's a big event."

"And it's probably going to be a big party, but I didn't want to leave anyone off the list," Kenna said. "And then Daniel's mom added a few more names. We've been delivering invitations all morning, so if you don't mind us coming in, I know Jacob would enjoy some playtime with Oliver."

"Of course I don't mind." Harper stepped away from the door so that they could enter.

Kenna followed her into the living room, where they put the babies on the blanket already spread out on the floor and scattered with some of Oliver's favorite toys. Of course, Coco had to be right in the middle of everything, too.

"Can I get you something to drink?" Harper asked. "Lemonade or sweet tea?"

"Sweet tea would be nice," Kenna agreed.

Harper slipped out to the kitchen and returned with two tall glasses and a plate of cookies.

Kenna's glance lingered on the plate. "Are those my mother-in-law's snickerdoodles?"

"They are," Harper confirmed.

Kenna wrapped both hands around her glass as if to resist the temptation. "Those cookies are deliciously addictive."

"That's why I serve them to company—so that I don't

eat them all myself." She sipped her tea. "Have you ever seen our show when we've had Kane Holland on?"

"I never miss 'In the Kitchen with Kane,'" Kenna assured her.

"He did a favorite-cookies segment, and one of the recipes was snickerdoodles. But I have to admit, his weren't nearly as good as Jane Garrett's."

"You'll have to tell her that when you come to Jacob's birthday party next week." Kenna gave in and selected a cookie.

"Isn't the party a family thing?"

"Mostly," Kenna agreed. "But you're connected to Oliver and Oliver's connected to Ryan and Ryan is Daniel's cousin, which means that you're family, too."

The logic was convoluted, but because she liked Kenna, she was willing to be persuaded. "In that case, we'll be there."

"Good," she said.

"Kee?" Oliver said, abandoning his blocks and cars and toddling over to the table where she'd put the plate of cookies.

"Yes, you can have a cookie," Harper told him.

He took two from the plate, one in each fist.

"One for Jacob," she said, because she knew he'd eat both if he wasn't encouraged to share.

He toddled back over to Jacob and held one of the cookies toward his mouth, as if to feed it to him. His little friend didn't seem overly interested—until Coco snatched the treat out of Oliver's hand. Then, of course, Jacob started to cry, which made Oliver cry, too, and Coco—not understanding that she'd started the whole thing—began to bark.

Kenna picked up her son to settle him down, then sat him on her lap and offered him another cookie. Jacob took two tiny bites, then wriggled to get down so that he could go back to playing with Oliver, who was driving toy cars on the carpet. Coco sat on her butt, her eyes focused on the plate, her tail wagging hopefully.

Then the back door opened, and she raced in that direction, barking a happy greeting for Ryan, who had been outside cutting the grass.

Sure enough, when he came through the living room half a minute later, the puppy was dancing around his feet. "It's got to be ninety degrees out— Oh." He paused in the doorway when he saw Kenna sitting on the sofa.

Harper glanced at him, noting the way his broad shoulders strained the seams of his T-shirt, his hard body glistened with perspiration, and his square jaw was dark with stubble. He looked hot and sexy and just a little dangerous, and every nerve ending in her body tingled.

"I didn't realize we had company," he finished.

"I'm not company—I'm family," his cousin's wife reminded him.

Oliver, distracted by the sound of their conversation, had abandoned his play and raced to the doorway, lifting his arms toward Ryan. "Up."

Ryan took an instinctive step back. "Sorry, buddy—I need a shower first."

Oliver's brow furrowed. "Up," he insisted.

Harper crossed the room to intercept the little boy. "Uncle Ryan needs a bath," she explained, as he was more likely to understand *bath* than *shower*. "He's all sweaty and stinky."

But he wasn't really. Sweaty, yes—but not in a bad way. And not stinky at all. He smelled like a man who had been working outdoors, and the scent of sun-kissed male and fresh-cut grass wasn't unappealing. In fact, it was almost arousing.

Oliver tried to copy holding his nose. "Baff."

Ryan chuckled and rumpled his hair. "Yes, I'm going to have a bath," he promised.

Then his gaze shifted to Harper, skimmed over her from head to toe, making a different promise, and she felt as if it was ninety degrees *inside* the house.

"Excuse me, ladies," he said.

Harper set Oliver back down beside Jacob to resume his play. Kenna waited until she heard Ryan climb the stairs to the second level before she turned to her and said, "So how was it?"

"How was what?"

"Sex with Ryan."

Harper choked on her tea. "What?"

Her friend laughed. "Come on—the air was buzzing with electricity when he walked in here. And the way he looked at you…" She fanned her face with her hand.

Harper wished she had a fan herself as heat rushed into her cheeks. "Please tell me it isn't that obvious."

Kenna smiled. "I'm sorry, sweetie, but it's that obvious."

Harper was cleaning crumbs from the seat of Oliver's high chair when Ryan came back downstairs after his shower.

"Is Oliver down for his nap already?"

She nodded. "He was falling asleep in his chair."

He looked at the spotless table. "I guess I missed lunch?"

"There are a couple of sandwiches in the fridge."

He moved toward her, deliberately crowding her against the counter. "Do I smell better now?"

She inhaled deeply. "Mmm…you smell good," she confirmed. "But you really didn't smell so bad before."

"You said I was sweaty and stinky," he reminded her.

"I was trying to refrain from jumping you in front of your cousin's wife."

"Kenna knows the Garrett men are irresistible."

"Apparently." She moved past him and took the plate of sandwiches from the fridge, setting it on the table for him.

But he wasn't as interested in his lunch as he was curious about the reason for the obvious pique in her tone. He turned her to face him, looked at her questioningly.

"She guessed that we're sleeping together," Harper told him.

"And that bothers you?"

"A little." She moved back to the fridge to pour him a glass of lemonade, set it beside his plate.

He might have smiled at the domesticity of her actions if it hadn't been so apparent that she was upset. "Why does it bother you?"

"Maybe it wasn't that she figured it out so much as that she wasn't surprised. After all, what woman could resist Ryan Garrett for more than two days?"

"You held out for years," he felt compelled to point out.

"But in the end, I succumbed. Just like every other woman."

"There aren't any other women," he said, starting to realize what was bothering her.

"Not right now," she acknowledged. "But in all the years that I've known you, it seemed as if you were with a different woman every time our paths crossed."

"You can't really be upset that I went out with other women during a period of time in which you made it clear you weren't interested in going out with me."

"I can," she said. "I know it's not rational, but I can."

"Do you think you could maybe give me more of an explanation than that?"

She exhaled a frustrated breath. "You remind me of my father."

His brows lifted. "That's a little…disconcerting."

She smacked his shoulder. "I don't mean like that."

"What do you mean?"

"You're so effortlessly charming. You don't even have to try, and women fall at your feet." She looked pointedly at the floor, where Coco had plopped herself down by his toes and was looking up at him with adoring eyes. "Or maybe I should have said 'females of all species.'"

"Coco doesn't count—she loves everybody." He scooped up the dog, because he couldn't resist those eyes, and tucked her into the crook of his arm. The puppy exhaled a soft blissful sigh. "And I'm not your father, Harper. I wouldn't ever treat you—or any woman—the way your father has treated your mother."

"I know," she said. "Logically, I do know that. But it isn't always easy to be logical when you're involved with someone on a personal level."

It was the closest she'd ever come to admitting that she had feelings for him. He knew that she did, of course. Over the past couple of months, as they'd got to know one another better, they'd naturally grown closer—and the physical intimacy they shared was only one part of that.

He tipped her chin up and touched his mouth to hers. "That's okay—I don't mind if you're occasionally illogical. It proves you care about me."

"Of course I care about you."

He couldn't help but smile at the begrudging tone. It wasn't much of an admission of her feelings, but it was a start.

Chapter Twelve

Kenna and Daniel had a beautiful home on a larger-than-average-size lot, but the backyard didn't look nearly as spacious with the number of people who were milling around it.

Harper knew the birthday boy and Kenna and Daniel, of course, and Ryan's parents were there, too. But while several other faces looked familiar, she was at a complete loss to connect names with those faces.

"Those name tags would come in handy right about now," Harper said to Ryan, after Ellen stole Oliver away so they were free to mingle. At least that was the explanation the older woman had given for taking the little boy, but Harper suspected Ryan's mother was also worried about the upcoming custody hearing and wanted to spend every minute she could with him.

"You've met most of them before," he reminded her.

"Maybe," she acknowledged. "But there have to be close to fifty people here."

"Forty-three," Kenna said.

Harper turned to face her friend. "You said it was going to be mostly family."

"Thirty-four of them are family—thirty-one from the Garrett side."

"Wow—I guess our numbers really have expanded over the past few years," Ryan said.

"And they're still growing."

Ryan looked at her with raised eyebrows.

Kenna shook her head. "No. Not me. Not yet."

"Who?"

"Rachel and Andrew's baby is due in November and I just found out that Lukas and Julie are going to be parents again early in the New Year."

"Is there something in the water?" Harper wondered.

Her friend chuckled. "That's what Nate asked about Pinehurst, when Matt, Jack and Luke all hooked up with their respective spouses within a calendar year."

"Is that Matt over there—talking to Justin?" Ryan asked.

Kenna nodded. "He was coming down for a weeklong medical conference anyway, so he brought Georgia and the kids to visit with their North Carolina relatives."

Something must have caught the corner of her eye, because she turned her head slightly and nodded. "Daniel's signaling for me to bring out the burgers," she said. "Please—eat, drink and be merry. There are snacks on the tables, beverages in the coolers and dinner will be ready soon."

It was easy enough for Harper to identify Matthew, because Ryan had said he was talking to Justin. As for his wife, she didn't have a clue. "Which one is Georgia?"

"The one beside my cousin Tristyn."

"That would be helpful if I knew who Tristyn was."

"She's holding the baby in the pink overalls. But the baby—Kylie—belongs to her sister Lauryn. She's sitting on the swing with Maura—Andrew's daughter."

She remembered Maura from the funeral, because the little girl had spent a lot of time with Oliver. And wrestling on the ground beside Maura were two little boys, probably around eight years old. "Twins?"

Ryan followed her gaze, nodded. "Quinn and Shane—they're with Matt and Georgia."

"Oliver's enough of a handful some days—I can't imagine what we'd do if there were two of him."

"Actually, Matt and Georgia have four—the twins, Pippa and Aidan."

Harper looked at Georgia with a new respect. "How does she do it?"

"You'd have to ask her." He slid an arm across her shoulders. "Come on—I'll introduce you."

They spent a few minutes chatting with Georgia and her husband, when he came to join them. Harper was surprised to learn that Georgia had been married before and that only Aidan, the youngest, was Matt's biological child. Through further conversation with other people throughout the afternoon, she learned that Matt's brother Lukas had adopted his wife's son from a previous relationship, and Nathan's fiancée had a nine-year-old son from her first marriage.

No wonder Ryan hadn't balked at the idea of raising his best friend's orphaned little boy—he understood, probably far better than Harper did, not just the importance of family but that the definition was not limited by biology. The Garretts were made up of a lot of different pieces, but they all seemed to fit seamlessly together to make the whole. And as she mingled with Ryan, she wondered where she fit with the group—or if she could.

After everyone had eaten, Daniel carried out an enormous slab cake with *Happy 1st Birthday, Jacob* spelled out in blue letters. Kenna carried a matching oversize cupcake decorated simply with a number 1 on it and set it on the tray of Jacob's high chair.

The birthday boy looked from the cupcake to his audience, as if he wasn't quite sure why so many people had gathered to watch him eat his dessert. But as camera flashes went off, he smiled, clearly accustomed to the spotlight.

The baby shoved his hand into the cake, making a face as icing squished through his fingers. Then he bent over and put his mouth directly on the cake, so that icing smeared his nose and his chin. He looked up as another flash went off, then clapped his hands together, spraying icing in the process. By the time he had eaten his fill of the dessert, there was as much on his face and in his hair as had ended up in his mouth. And when he was done, his dad just scooped him out of the chair, stripped his clothes away and dunked him in a little plastic pool that had been set up for the little ones to play in.

While he was doing that, Kenna cut up the big cake for the rest of their guests. Oliver, unwilling to wait for cake, was eyeing the remnants of a fruit platter on the picnic table. His hand was curled in a fist and, judging by the color of the juice that dripped down his arm, he'd already snatched a piece of watermelon from the tray.

Before Harper could take a step in that direction, Ryan's mother was there. Ellen guided Oliver's hand to his mouth, encouraging him to eat the fruit. Then she unfurled his fingers and carefully wiped each one on a paper napkin.

The little boy was in good hands with Ryan's family—competent, caring and loving hands. He was one of those pieces she'd been thinking about earlier. As soon as he'd become part of Ryan's life, he'd been accepted as part of theirs by the rest of the Garrett clan. Harper was grateful to know that although he'd lost his parents, he'd grow up with a strong sense of family, of knowing he belonged.

Yes, she was pleased for Oliver—and just the tiniest bit envious.

"You've been quiet since we got back," Ryan said to Harper, after they'd returned from the party and settled Oliver into bed.

"I was just thinking."

"About anything in particular?"

"About how lucky you are to be part of such a close-knit family."

"I was lucky to steal some cake to bring home in a crowd that size," he agreed, peeling the plastic wrap off the plate and nudging it across the table toward her.

"No, thanks."

He retrieved a fork from the drawer. "You didn't have any at the party."

"I'm not really a fan of cake."

He stared at her as if he couldn't believe what she'd said. "It's cake—it's soft, it's sweet, it's delicious. What's not to like?"

The thousand calories per bite, but of course, she wasn't going to admit that to him.

"Try it." He waved the fork near her mouth. "And don't you dare say you don't like chocolate, because I've seen the stash of Godiva chocolate bars in the back of the freezer."

"Why would you open a container marked 'quinoa'?"

"Because I didn't know what quinoa was and I was hungry."

"Did you eat my chocolate?"

"Your stash is safe," he assured her. "So long as you tell me why you don't want a piece of Jacob's birthday cake."

"I filled up on other stuff."

"You had a hamburger without a bun and about two tablespoons of broccoli salad."

"Why are you so preoccupied with what I eat?"

"Because you are."

She shrugged. "Lifelong habits are hard to break."

"You're not old enough to have lifelong habits," he chided.

"I was a catalog model for designer children's clothing before I was two years old."

"No kidding?"

"No kidding," she confirmed.

His lips curved. "So I'm dating a model?"

She rolled her eyes. "Hardly."

"Ex-model, then."

"Ex-ex-ex," she said. "And you could probably add a few more exes considering that my career in front of the camera ended when I was nine."

"What happened?"

"I took a tumble while skiing and tore the ACL in my right knee, after which I had surgery and then spent six weeks not able to do much of anything. I gained eight pounds and the company hired another girl for their catalog. My mother was furious and that was the end of my illustrious career in front of the camera."

"Good for your mother," he said, "pulling you out of the business."

She managed a wry smile. "My mother was my agent. She didn't pull me out—she put me on a diet. No fat, no sugar, no starch."

"You're kidding."

She shook her head.

"That explains a lot about your eating habits," he noted.

"I like salad," she said, just a little defensively.

Ryan made a face. "Nobody likes salad that much."

"When I finally lost the extra weight, I promised myself I wouldn't put it back on."

And she obviously hadn't, because she was all angles now. He shook his head. "I'm sorry—I'm still trying to get over the fact that your mother put you, at nine years of age, on a diet because you'd gained eight pounds."

"She lives and works in a world where people are judged as much by how they look as what they do."

"Is that why you left New York City?"

"I think that's probably why I chose to work behind the camera," she admitted. "Because even after four years of therapy, I still wondered if I wasn't pretty enough, skinny enough or talented enough to do anything else. And because I'm in control there. Because I've proven that I'm smart enough, organized enough and committed enough to make *Coffee Time* the number one–rated show on WNCC."

"You should be proud of everything you've accomplished," he told her sincerely. "And some people should not have kids."

She looked away. "I know."

He tipped her chin up, forcing her to meet his gaze. "I was referring to your mother, not you."

"But she's the only example I ever had—can you see now why I'm so worried about screwing up with Oliver? I don't want to be the reason he's in therapy in high school."

"You've got my family now," he reminded her.

"Your family is great," she admitted.

"And they love you."

Her gaze skittered away again. "That's not a word that you should just throw around like that."

"Like what?"

"Like it's…easy."

"Loving someone is easy," he told her.

And it always had been in his family. Not that everything was always hearts and flowers, but he'd never had any doubt that his parents loved each other and their kids. Even when he'd fought with his brothers, as was inevitable with sibling relationships, he wouldn't hesitate to call on either of them—or any of his cousins—if he needed anything, and he felt confident that they would do the same.

Harper hadn't grown up with that same kind of unconditional support, and he hated to think that those who should have bolstered her self-confidence and self-worth had managed to do just the opposite.

Maybe she wasn't actually perfect. In fact, he'd be the first to admit that she was a little uptight and a lot demanding. She was also beautiful and warm and giving. She always committed 100 percent to whatever task was assigned to her—not just at work but in life.

She'd been devastated by the loss of her best friend and then expected to take on the responsibility of raising her child. It would have been simple enough for her to say that she didn't want to do it. Instead she'd accepted the challenge.

And he knew it had been a challenge. He wouldn't have thought it was possible for anyone to have less experience with babies than he had, but it had been apparent to both of them that Harper won that contest hands down. She hadn't had the first clue what to do with Oliver, but she'd learned. Even when she'd been beyond exhausted, he'd see her reading over books on child care or researching toddler menus on the internet.

She wasn't perfect, but sometime over the past two months he'd decided that she was perfect for *him*.

He knew it was going to take some time before she was ready to hear it, before she let herself trust his feelings—

and her own. So for now he put the empty cake plate aside and took her upstairs to show her—loving her slowly, tenderly and thoroughly.

Ryan glanced up at the knock—and bark—at the door to see his brother standing there with Coco on her pink leash, her tail wagging ecstatically.

"Look at you," he said to the puppy. "I swear you've grown three inches in the past three days." Then, to his brother, "Why didn't I get the memo about bring-your-dog-to-work day?"

Braden didn't respond to his attempted humor. "It turns out that Dana's allergic to dogs."

He lifted a brow. "And you didn't know that?"

His brother looked away, making Ryan suspect that his sister-in-law's excuse for not wanting to keep the puppy was just that—an excuse.

"How bad are her allergies?" he asked. "Because I know Jordyn has to take an antihistamine every day to live with that ugly cat of hers."

"I don't know how bad," Braden admitted. "But aside from the allergies, she accused me of patronizing her—expecting a dog to take the place of the child she hasn't been able to have."

"Is that why you got the puppy?"

"Not to take the place of a child," Braden denied, squatting down to scratch Coco's head. "But maybe I wanted to see if she could focus on anything other than her obsession to have a baby."

"She still won't consider adoption?"

His brother shook his head. "She's so screwed up from her father's abandonment of his family that she's determined to figure out a way for us to have a baby that is truly ours so that she can have a real family again."

Ryan could hear the frustration in his brother's voice, and although he wanted to help, he didn't know that anyone could. The baby issue was something Braden and Dana had to figure out for themselves. "What do *you* want?"

"I want to hear her laugh again, to remember the woman I fell in love with. The past three years have been an endless cycle of anger and tears, and I honestly don't know how much longer I can do it." He stroked the puppy's fur in a gesture that Ryan suspected was as much apology as affection. "And it doesn't help that there are babies crawling all over the place at every family gathering."

Over the past year, Ryan had noticed that Dana was uncharacteristically subdued whenever they were all together, and then she'd simply stopped showing up for family events. In fact, when Lauryn had given birth to Kylie in early March, Braden had visited them at the hospital but his wife had been conspicuously absent. "Does she know that Rachel's pregnant?"

Braden's brows lifted. "*I* didn't know that Rachel was pregnant."

Ryan winced. "It's recent news—I'm sure Andrew just hasn't had a chance to tell everyone yet."

"Or he doesn't know how to tell me, because he knows we've been struggling to start a family for so long."

Unable to refute his brother's logic, Ryan opted to redirect the conversation. "What are you going to do with Coco now?"

"I guess I have to take her back to the SPCA," Braden said.

"Take her back—as if she was an ill-fitting sweater?"

"I know it's not an ideal solution, but I'm sure she won't be there more than a day or two before another family takes her home."

"And you don't think four different homes in the space of a week will traumatize her at all?"

Braden winced. "I wanted to keep her. I thought for sure Dana would warm up to her in time. But this morning, she said that her allergies were really bothering her and I had to choose between her and the puppy."

"There you go—you do have options."

"You do know that's my wife you're talking about?"

"Yeah, sorry," Ryan said, although he wasn't sure if he was apologizing for the insensitive remark or his brother's marital status.

"I don't want to take her back to the shelter," Braden said.

He nodded, because he knew it was true. If his brother had wanted to take Coco back, he wouldn't have detoured to his office.

Ryan crouched down in front of his desk and the puppy immediately scrambled toward him, planting her front paws on his knees so that she could reach up to lick his face.

"I don't think she'd be traumatized if she went back to your house," Braden remarked.

"As Harper pointed out, a baby is enough responsibility without adding a baby dog to the mix." And there was no doubting the validity of her argument.

On the other hand, he couldn't help remembering how she'd laughed watching Oliver and Coco play together; how she'd liked to watch TV in the evenings with the puppy cuddled in her lap; and how sad she'd looked when they'd dropped Coco off at Braden's house three days earlier.

Coco leaned in closer, nuzzling her face against his throat, and he sighed. "I'll take her home tonight—but I'm not making any promises."

When Ryan got home, Oliver was playing on the kitchen floor, banging on a pot with a wooden spoon while Harper sautéed green beans.

She glanced over her shoulder when she heard the door open. "Dinner's almost..." The words trailed off when she saw the puppy in his arms.

Oliver spotted his furry bundle at the same time, dropping his spoon and scrambling to his feet. "Coco! Woof!"

The puppy obliged by woofing in response.

Ryan set her down on the floor. Harper shook her head and sighed.

"The anniversary surprise didn't go over as well as Braden anticipated," he told her.

"And now we have a puppy," she guessed.

"You could say no."

She looked at the boy and dog, then back at Ryan. "As if."

"I wouldn't have chosen to get him a dog at this stage, either," Ryan admitted. "But I think Coco's good for him. For all of us."

"Sure. Chasing a puppy all over the house will be a welcome distraction from worrying about the custody hearing hanging over our heads."

"I knew you'd see the bright side."

She dumped the green beans into a bowl and shoved it in his direction.

Chapter Thirteen

"That was a waste of time," Ryan commented as he sat down beside Harper in Shelly Watts's office Tuesday afternoon.

He hadn't known what to expect, but he'd hoped that the Renforths would agree that Oliver was being well taken care of in accordance with his parents' wishes and be persuaded to withdraw their claim for custody. That hadn't happened.

"Mediation is a useful tool for settling disputes, but both parties have to be willing to compromise for it to be successful," the attorney said.

"I thought our proposal for visitation was reasonable," Harper said.

"It was more than reasonable," the attorney agreed. "But Aubrey and Jeremy are insisting that they don't want visitation—they want custody."

And although a guardian *ad litem* had been appointed

by the court as an independent advocate for Oliver's best interests, certain statements made by the attorney during her visit led Ryan to believe she had a bias toward children being placed with biological family members whenever possible. In addition, she'd made no effort to hide her disapproval of the fact that the little boy's parents had chosen guardians who were unmarried.

"So what happens now?" he asked Shelly.

"Now we wait for a trial date," she told them.

"How long will that take?"

"It depends on how much time the clerk thinks will be required and how many other cases are on the docket."

"Weeks? Months?"

"Yes," Shelly said unhelpfully. "It could be as soon as a couple of weeks or as long as several months."

"What are we supposed to do in the meantime?" Ryan asked.

"Exactly what you have been doing."

"Do you think…? Is there any chance…?" Harper's question trailed off, and Ryan knew she was reluctant to even articulate the fear that they might lose Oliver.

"I wish I could give you a guarantee, but I can't," Shelly said. "While it seems unlikely that any judge would award custody to a couple who has had no contact with the child until a few weeks ago, it's not outside the realm of possibility, especially considering that Aubrey shares a biological connection with Oliver."

"But it isn't what Melissa and Darren wanted," Harper said, sounding close to tears.

"And we'll make sure the judge is aware of their wishes," Shelly promised.

"Isn't there something else we can do?" Ryan asked.

"You've done everything you can. You've both made a dedicated effort to do what's best for Oliver, and I can't see any reason why the judge would rule against your application."

"But you can't guarantee that he won't." Harper echoed the lawyer's words.

"Every judge has his or her own personal biases," Shelly warned. "It's possible that a judge might decide that the biological tie between Oliver and Aubrey carries more weight than anything else. It's also possible that a judge might favor the stability of a traditional marital relationship."

"That's not fair," Harper protested.

"I'm not saying either of those factors will come into play—I'm just letting you know that they might."

"Well, we obviously can't manufacture a biological connection," Ryan noted. "But we could get married."

Shelly sat back in her chair and folded her hands on her desk, her gaze shifting between her clients. "Is that something you've considered?"

Ryan reached for Harper's hand and linked their fingers together, squeezing gently in a silent plea for her cooperation. "I haven't had a chance to formally propose, but it's something I've—we've—been thinking about."

He hoped the lawyer didn't notice the tiny furrow that appeared between Harper's brows as she squeezed his hand back, almost painfully hard.

"Hypothetically, I can tell you that a legal union between the child's named guardians would provide the court with evidence of stability," Shelly said cautiously. "However, I cannot advocate a marriage solely for the purpose of bolstering your case for custody."

"Of course not," Ryan agreed.

"You can let me know if you decide to take steps in that direction," Shelly said. "And I'll let you know as soon as we have a hearing date."

They thanked the attorney and walked out of her office, still holding hands.

But as soon as they were outside the building, Harper turned to him. "Are you insane?" she demanded.

"Are you referring to my proposal?"

"If by *proposal* you mean your asinine suggestion that we should get married to strengthen our case for custody of Oliver, then yes."

"Then the answer is no—I'm not insane. And if you take a minute to think about it, you'll realize the idea isn't just sane but rational," he insisted. "We're both committed to raising Oliver, because that's what Melissa and Darren wanted us to do, but showing the court that we're equally as committed to one another might be the only way to ensure we get to keep their son."

"Why can't we just trust the judge to see that we're the best option for Oliver?"

"Because we don't get a second chance if he decides against us."

She nibbled on her lip, unable to deny that fact but apparently not yet convinced to go along with his plan.

"Think about it," he urged. "Marriage would simply be a formalization of our current arrangement. And it would make things easier for Oliver, too, if we were married. Especially when he starts school and gets involved in extracurricular activities."

"How do you figure?"

"Instead of a teacher trying to connect Mr. Garrett and Ms. Ross to Oliver Cannon, it would just be Mr. and Mrs. Garrett and Oliver."

"So not only am I supposed to marry you, I'm supposed to take your name?"

He held up his hands. "Your choice."

She huffed out a breath. "Maybe we could just get engaged."

He shook his head. "An engagement is easily broken."

"So are marriage vows."

Although he understood why she was wary, he couldn't let her hide behind her fears. "But the exchange of vows shows a deeper commitment than an engagement ring."

"Marriage is supposed to be sacred," she said. "Despite the mockery my parents make of it, I know that. And I promised myself that I would never take that step with someone unless I truly believed the marriage could last."

"I will honor my vows," he assured her.

"Except for the 'love' part."

She sounded almost wistful, as if she *wanted* him to love her. And he considered—for the briefest of moments—telling her that he did. But while he'd recently begun to acknowledge and accept the depth of his feelings for her, he knew Harper wasn't ready to do the same. Instead he said only, "Maybe sharing a life and raising a child together will lead us to fall in love."

"That's a big maybe."

"It's not a decision I can make alone," he told her. "We both have to be committed to making it work. I know that I am, because I'm prepared to do whatever is necessary to honor Darren and Melissa's wishes for their child."

Not surprisingly, her chin lifted. "And you think I'm not?"

"I don't know if you are—are you willing to marry me?"

"If you really think that's our best option."

"I do," he confirmed. "I know it doesn't guarantee a judgment in our favor, but it can't hurt."

"Then I guess we're getting married."

"When?"

"I'm free for the rest of the day," she said.

He stared at her for a minute, trying to decide if she was serious. "We can't get married today."

"Actually, we can," she told him. "In North Carolina, a marriage license is valid as soon as it's issued—there's no waiting period required."

"How do you know that?"

"We did a live proposal and wedding on *Coffee Time with Caroline* for Valentine's Day."

"What if the proposal had been refused?"

"We had a backup plan," she told him.

"Of course you did," he mused.

"So—are we going to get married today?"

"No."

Her brows rose. "You've changed your mind?"

"No," he said again. "Because I don't know about your mom and dad, but I know mine would never forgive me if they weren't invited to my wedding."

"I thought we were just getting married, not having a wedding."

"And the difference is?" he asked curiously.

"Witnesses."

He fought against a smile. "It's not legal if you don't have witnesses."

"Okay—the number of witnesses," she clarified.

"You don't want your family to come to the wedding," he guessed.

He'd never met either of her parents, but he'd heard enough about them to understand why she'd moved away from New York. And while he didn't believe they'd ever put her needs above their own, he had to believe that they would make the effort to attend their only daughter's wedding.

"I don't want my mother pointing out that I should play

up my cleavage to draw attention from my hips or my father hitting on a bridesmaid or my brother getting drunk—but other than that, why not?"

"And suddenly I find myself anticipating the holidays with my in-laws."

"Be careful what you wish for," she told him.

"Getting back to a wedding date," he said. "How's Saturday?"

"You're getting married on Saturday," Kenna repeated, as she examined the gorgeous marquise-cut diamond on Harper's finger. "As in *this* Saturday?"

It was Wednesday afternoon and Harper had asked the other woman if she was available to meet for lunch between her classes. As it turned out, there was a school-wide assembly after lunch, so Kenna wasn't just available but willing to play hooky for the rest of the afternoon.

Harper nodded.

"Isn't that rushing things a little?"

"You eloped in Las Vegas only hours after Daniel proposed."

"Because Daniel needed to be married to gain access to his trust fund."

That was a part of the story that Harper hadn't heard. "That's why you married him?"

"No, that's why *he* married *me*. I married him for a hundred thousand dollars," Kenna said, then laughed at the surprise on Harper's face. "And then we fell in love."

"Well, we're getting married because Ryan believes that a wedding will increase our chances of retaining custody of Oliver."

"Is that the only reason?" her friend asked, sounding disappointed.

"It's the only reason," she confirmed.

Kenna didn't look convinced. "And how do you expect to put a wedding together in three days?"

"It's just going to be a small and informal ceremony."

"Uh-huh," Kenna said, sounding amused.

"That's what Ryan and I agreed."

"So what time and where is this small and informal ceremony taking place?" her friend asked.

"I'm not sure," Harper admitted.

Kenna's brows lifted.

"Ryan's mom said she would take care of the details."

"And she'll be happy to do it," Kenna assured her. "Just don't be surprised if it's not nearly as small or informal as you're expecting."

"She did say I should buy a new dress," Harper admitted. "And ask a friend to stand up with me."

"I'd be happy to go shopping with you."

"I'd appreciate that. I'd be even more grateful if you'd be my matron of honor."

"Of course," her friend agreed. "But now we definitely need to go shopping, because I want a new dress, too."

"I think we should get rid of the veil," Harper said, gazing critically at her reflection in the small mirror as she waited for her cue to walk down the aisle of the courthouse chapel.

Kenna stood behind her, looking over her shoulder. "Why?"

"I think it's too formal for the dress."

"I like it," her matron of honor said. "Plus, it's Ryan's mom's, so it covers the 'something borrowed' requirement of the poem."

Harper had been touched that Ellen wanted her to wear the delicate lace headpiece for the wedding and she hadn't

wanted to offend Ryan's mother by declining. But now…
somehow the veil changed everything.

"It would be easier to pretend it wasn't a real wedding if
you didn't actually look like a bride, wouldn't it?" Kenna's
soft question showed surprising—and unerring—insight.

"That's part of it," Harper admitted.

"If you're freaking out over a veil, how are you going
to handle the vows?" her friend asked.

"I'm not freaking out," she denied. "Why would I freak
out over an intimate gathering of family and friends?"

It was supposed to be a hypothetical question, to reas-
sure her that there was no need to freak out.

Then the door to the anteroom opened and a familiar
voice rang out. "There's my baby girl."

And flashbulbs exploded in her face.

Saturday afternoon, Ryan stood beside Justin, his brother
and best man, at the front of the chapel, waiting to exchange
vows with Harper.

And waiting.

About fifty people were seated on the pew-style benches
in the gallery. The majority of the guests were family,
mostly his, with a few friends and work colleagues mixed
in here and there.

"It's four-oh-two," Justin said close to his ear. "Maybe
she decided to pull a runaway bride."

Ryan shook his head. "Not Harper." And definitely not
with Oliver's future at stake.

The back doors of the courtroom opened and Ryan's
heart started to race. But it wasn't Harper who stepped into
the room—or even Kenna, who, as matron of honor, would
precede the bride. Instead it was half a dozen photographers with various press credentials hanging around their

necks and cameras clasped in their hands as they jockeyed for position.

He wouldn't have guessed that Charisma had paparazzi, but somehow word had got out that soap star Peter Ross was going to be in town for his daughter's wedding and they'd tracked him down here.

Ryan swore softly under his breath.

"I didn't know your fiancée was some kind of celebrity," Justin said.

"She's not," Ryan denied. "Her father is."

"I thought her parents couldn't be here for the wedding."

That was the response Harper had expected when she'd sent the email to inform them of the event, and it was the response she'd received. He'd wanted her to call, suggesting that the news warranted a more personal form of communication, but his fiancée had insisted that emailing would alleviate any awkward silences while her parents tried to explain why they were unable to attend their only daughter's wedding.

She'd accepted their rejection of the invitation with aplomb; he hadn't been able or willing to do so.

"Obviously there was a change of plans," Ryan told his brother, not wanting to reveal the part he'd played in getting them there.

The doors opened again and a stylish fiftysomething woman and a much younger man walked in. The woman could only be Harper's mother, Gayle Everton-Ross, and the man her brother, Spencer. Cameras whirred and clicked as they took their seats in the front row.

When they were settled, the clerk started the recorded music and Kenna appeared. And then, finally, Harper was there, and the sight of her actually stole the breath from Ryan's lungs.

She wore a white dress. Not a wedding gown but a casual summer dress with tiny little straps over her shoulders and a flirty skirt that fell just above her knees. Her slender legs were bare and her feet were tucked into sexy sandals that tied up around her ankles and added at least three inches to her height.

Her hair was pulled away from her face in some kind of fancy knot and was topped with a short layered veil that he recognized from photos of his mom and dad's wedding. In her hands, she carried a hand-tied bouquet of creamy white tulips.

"I guess I was wrong about the runaway part," Justin mused beside him.

Ryan was glad, because he knew that if she ran, he would run after her. And not just for Oliver's sake.

Harper had agreed to this wedding for the little boy, and Ryan couldn't deny that he'd deliberately played that card because he knew it would trump any arguments she might have made against his proposal. What he hadn't told her—what he knew she wasn't ready to hear—was that he *wanted* this marriage. He wanted her in his life for the long term, not just because Oliver needed her but because he did, too.

Behind the courthouse was a modest green space with wrought iron benches, urns overflowing with colorful flowers and a three-tiered marble fountain. Though not originally designed for the purpose, the area had become a popular reception location for those who married in the courthouse chapel. Of course, Ellen Garrett had gone one step up from a potluck set out on folding tables and had arranged for seating under cover of an enormous white tent. There was a buffet table where hot and cold hors d'oeuvres were served along with tall glasses of nonalcoholic champagne.

After their formal wedding photos were taken—including, as a gift from the bride to her matron of honor, a picture of Kenna with Brock Lawrie, aka the father of the bride. It was only when Ryan spotted Daniel returning from the courthouse with Jacob that he realized he'd lost sight of Oliver. There were enough people around that he was sure the little boy was being watched by someone, but that certainty didn't dispel the unease that churned in his gut.

"Do you see Oliver?" he asked his dad.

John glanced around. "No," he said, unconcerned.

Ryan scanned the gathering again, but he didn't see him. His mother was talking to Aunt Jane; Harper's mother had her cell phone pressed to her ear; and Oliver obviously wasn't with either of them.

Then he spotted his cousin Jordyn walking near the fountain, and he exhaled a sigh of relief to see Oliver's little hand firmly clasped in hers. They were headed back toward the tent, and he met them halfway.

"He's a little wet," Jordyn said apologetically. "I didn't quite catch him before he started splashing."

Ryan wasn't concerned about the water—his attention was focused on something else. He crouched down in front of Oliver and gestured to the beanbag dog that was clutched in his hand. "Where did you get that?" he asked.

Of course, the child's limited vocabulary didn't allow him to answer the question. He responded only with, "Woof."

"It does look like Woof, doesn't it?" he agreed.

Almost identical, in fact, right down to the ragged ears that Oliver liked to chew on.

"Ryan?" Jordyn looked at him worriedly. "What's wrong?"

He stood up again. "Was anyone else with Oliver by the fountain?"

"No. He was by himself, playing in the water."

"Do me a favor?" he asked her. "Don't mention this to Harper."

"Don't mention what to Harper?"

He shook his head. "Just...that I had a moment of panic when I didn't know where he was."

"I won't," Jordyn agreed. "But I am going to go say goodbye to your bride now because I have to head into work in a couple of hours."

"Thanks for coming," he said.

"I had to come." She smiled and kissed his cheek. "I wouldn't have believed you were married if I hadn't witnessed it myself."

When Jordyn had gone, he lifted Oliver onto his hip and carried him back to the tent. "I think you're more than a little wet," he said. "Let's see what we can do about that."

He found a towel in the bottom of the diaper bag—he wasn't sure why there was a towel in there, but Harper insisted on ensuring the bag was stocked with all kinds of things Ryan didn't think the baby would ever need—and rubbed the front of the little boy's shirt.

"Woof's pretty wet, too," he said. "What do you think? Should we dry him off?"

Oliver held tight. Then he spied a snack-size container of Cheerios in one of the side pockets of the diaper bag and dropped the toy in pursuit of the cereal. Ryan sat him down on a chair and opened the lid.

He didn't want to consider that this beanbag puppy could be the same one that the boy had lost weeks ago and miles away, but the possibility that Oliver just happened to "find" an identical dog was too unbelievable. It wasn't just a coincidence—it was downright creepy.

When he was certain that the little boy was thoroughly focused on his snack, Ryan picked up the toy and tossed it in the nearest trash can.

Harper was, surprisingly, a little disappointed when the limo returned to whisk her parents and brother back to the airport. Although she hadn't appreciated all of the fanfare that had arrived with them, she was glad that they'd been there. And walking down the aisle with her dad had meant more to her than she'd expected—and his strong presence kept her steady when she saw Ryan Garrett waiting for her at the front of the chapel.

Her groom. Her husband. For better or for worse.

"Thank you," she said, brushing her lips against his cheek.

"For what?"

"For guilting them into coming."

"It didn't take much," he said. "They wanted to be here."

"Yes, my mother made a point of saying that nothing could have kept her away from her only daughter's first wedding."

"*First* wedding?"

She nodded. "And when I told her that I was hoping it would be my only wedding, she—looking amused—said, 'Well, all the more reason for us to be here, then.'

"As if I didn't know that the real reason was to get another picture of my dad in the papers, along with mention of his upcoming projects."

"How did the press know they would be here?"

She sighed. "My mother sent out a press release."

He slipped his arms around her. "I'm flattered that she thought the event newsworthy enough."

"Only because my father walked me down the aisle—

which, again, explains why he was here to walk me down the aisle."

His lips curved. "And you say I'm cynical."

"No one in my family does anything without ulterior motives," she warned him.

"So what was yours for marrying me?" he challenged.

"You know what it was—to bolster our claim for custody of Oliver."

"That was the *real* motive," he clarified. "I want to know what nefarious plans are lurking beneath the surface."

"I don't have any nefarious plans."

"Oh." He sounded disappointed. "Not even to take me to your bed and seduce me?"

"Well, that idea does hold some appeal," she acknowledged.

"I'd rather you held on to me," he told her.

She linked her hands behind his neck. "How's this?"

"It's a good start." He pulled her closer to his body. "This is better."

She tilted her head back, a wordless invitation that he didn't hesitate to accept. As his lips moved over hers, she melted against the hard strength of his body. His hands slid up her back and down again, and she shivered against him.

He eased his mouth from hers. "What would you say if I suggested we go home and consummate this marriage?"

She smiled. "I'd say 'Let's go.'"

Chapter Fourteen

They'd intended to send a copy of their marriage certificate to their lawyer, but it turned out that they didn't need to. Shelly called on Monday to congratulate them, having read about their nuptials in the morning paper. Apparently having the paparazzi at their wedding had served a useful purpose after all.

Shelly promised to amend their response to reflect their now-married status. And when Caroline did her weekend summary on *Coffee Time*, she included congratulations to the happy couple.

Aside from the temporary notoriety and the rings on her finger, not much else changed in their relationship after the wedding. And that was okay, because Harper was content with everything exactly as it was. She had a great job, a comfortable home, a beautiful little boy, an adorable—and slightly hyperactive—puppy and a husband who ensured that she never regretted the sleep she lost in his bed. The only thing that could possibly make her happier would be to have Oliver's custody settled, but she refused to let the threat of that hearing interfere with her enjoyment of every day.

"Diya—do you have the contact info for that teacher who started the after-school community service program that we want to spotlight next month?"

"I've got something better," her assistant said from the doorway. "Your husband."

"My—" Harper looked up, surprised—and pleased—to see Ryan standing in the doorway. "Oh, hi."

He smiled. "Hi."

Diya nudged him past the door, then slipped out, closing it firmly behind her.

"You've never stopped by the studio before."

"And I might never again," he warned. "This place is an obstacle course through chaos."

"There's a lot going on," she agreed.

"Well, I'm not going to take up much of your time," he promised. "I just wanted to stop by to invite you to dinner tonight."

"We have dinner together every night," she pointed out.

"Tonight I want to take you out."

"Like…on a date?"

"Yes, on a date," he confirmed.

"Why?" she asked.

"Because it occurred to me that, despite having been married for almost a week, we've never actually been on a date. I'd like to remedy that."

"Just the two of us?"

"That's what makes it a date," he confirmed.

"What about Oliver?"

"My parents are going to keep him. And the puppy. Overnight."

"Sounds…promising."

"Is that a yes?"

"Where are you taking me?"

"Casa Mercado."

Her brows lifted at his mention of the upscale tapas bar and restaurant that had opened about six months earlier. "I appreciate the gesture, but you do realize that with the promise of an empty house, I'd probably put out for a burger and fries from a drive-through window?"

"I'll keep that in mind for future reference," he said. "Tonight we're going to Casa Mercado."

She had a date with her husband.

The idea made Harper strangely nervous.

They'd been living together for almost three months, sharing a bed for five weeks and married for six days, but tonight was their first real date.

She pampered herself in anticipation of the occasion, indulging in a leisurely soak in the tub and rubbing scented lotion on her skin. She couldn't remember the last time she'd dressed up in anticipation of being undressed, but she was optimistic that her husband would appreciate the black lace demicup bra and bikini panties that she wore beneath her little black dress even more than the dress itself.

She loved the way Ryan touched her. The way his hands stroked over her body, the way his lips caressed her skin. He knew all of her most sensitive spots and just where to linger. She really liked it when he lingered.

She kept waiting for the attraction to wane. It was inevitable. The extreme heights of emotion that characterized the beginning of any relationship couldn't last. She understood that, and she was prepared for it. She loved being with him, and she loved making love with him, but she wasn't *in* love with him and she certainly didn't expect that their marriage would turn into some happily-ever-after.

They'd married for Oliver's sake—to support their application for custody of their friends' little boy and because they'd promised to raise the child together. Their personal relationship was something else entirely and she had no illusions. But she was going to enjoy every minute that she had with him to ensure that she didn't have any regrets when it was over.

She was slipping her feet into her shoes when Ryan came into what had been "her" room and was now "their" bedroom. He halted in midstride, his eyes skimming her from head to toe and back again. "Mrs. Garrett, you look... Wow."

She eyed him up and down, appreciating the way the dark suit fit his long, lean body. "You look pretty good yourself, Mr. Garrett."

He settled his hands on her hips, drew her close. "What are you wearing underneath that dress?"

She tipped her head back and nipped playfully at his chin. "If you play your cards right, you'll find out later," she promised.

His hands slid around her back, over the curve of her buttocks. "Maybe I changed my mind about going out."

She put her hands on his chest and pushed him away. "You said we had an eight o'clock reservation at Casa Mercado."

"I did. We do. But suddenly, I'm thinking pizza—"

"I'm thinking you might need a little more than pizza to keep up your energy later."

He offered his arm. "Your wish is my command."

Ryan led Harper through an elaborate metal scrollwork archway into a walled courtyard that housed an outdoor bar/patio. The floor was an elaborate design of traditional Spanish tiles in burnt orange, warm gold and cobalt blue. The atmosphere was casual, with wooden chairs and tables and oversize market-style umbrellas in the same bright blue, and contemporary music spilled out of speakers hidden by the towering plants.

Walking through another archway, they left the courtyard patio and entered a quieter lounge space with dark-tiled floors, rustic wood-beam ceilings and arched entranceways. Where outside, everything had been color, inside was much more subdued. The tables were set with white linens, square plates, gleaming silver and a trio of tea-light candles in poppy-red glass holders. On the walls hung oversize sepiatoned photos of flamenco dancers, the monochromatic color scheme of each one set off by a splash of color—a red rose in a dancer's hair, glossy ruby-painted lips, a swirling skirt of bold crimson.

It was lucky that Ryan had made a reservation, because there weren't any empty tables in view. After they were seated, before they'd even had a chance to look at the wine list, a waitress appeared with a bottle of champagne and two flute glasses.

"Compliments of Chef Felipe, with congratulations on your recent marriage."

"Thank you," Ryan said. Then, when the wine had been poured and the waitress had gone, he looked questioningly at Harper. "Chef Felipe?"

"He was a guest on *Coffee Time* a few months back, right before the restaurant's grand opening. He made this amazing custard—*crema catalana*—on the air and sent little dishes of it around to everyone on the set."

"Was it good?"

"I practically licked the bowl."

His eyes darkened. "I would have enjoyed seeing that—you can be quite creative with your tongue."

Her cheeks flushed. "And then I did an extra circuit at the gym."

"We're definitely going to save room for dessert."

Between sips of the wine they nibbled on marinated black olives and shared bites of chorizo sautéed in white wine and fried potatoes in spicy tomato sauce. They also sampled piquillo peppers stuffed with Manchego cheese, bacon-wrapped dates drizzled with honey, mixed greens with pears and walnuts—because, as Ryan teasingly remarked, it wouldn't be a meal for Harper without some kind of salad—and chunks of Black Angus sirloin with a sweet mustard sauce.

They were almost finished their meal when the chef made his way to their table. He greeted Harper warmly and introduced himself to Ryan. "I apologize for not coming out sooner, but the kitchen was busy tonight."

"I imagine that makes you very happy," Harper said.

"It does," he confirmed. "And how was everything at your table? Were your tapas exceptional?"

"Yes, they were," Ryan confirmed.

Felipe nodded. "Our goal is to ensure that no customer leaves hungry or unhappy. The bigger challenge, for any new restaurant, is getting them in the door." He looked at Harper again. "You helped make that happen."

"Caroline made that happen—I didn't do anything," she denied.

"As a chef, I know the most important people are those who work behind the scenes," he told her. "So thank you."

"You're welcome."

"Now I must get back to the kitchen to make sure your *crema catalana* is absolutely fabulous."

"I guess we're having dessert," Ryan said as the other man walked away.

"I really don't think I can eat another bite and stay in this dress."

Her husband smiled. "Then let's take the *crema catalana* home and get you out of it."

So they did, and he did, and a long while later, they fell asleep together.

On Father's Day, they made another trek to the cemetery with Oliver. This second visit was, thankfully, a little less emotional than the first. Ryan's relationship with Harper had undergone some significant changes in the interim, and he knew their friends would be happy for both of them and pleased that they were committed to raising Oliver as a family.

Later that day, they went to his parents' house for the traditional Father's Day barbecue. His mother presided over the grill, basting and turning pieces of chicken and racks of ribs. She'd also made mashed potatoes, baked beans and steamed corn. Harper contributed a green salad, dinner rolls and a Rocky Road cheesecake that she picked up from The Sweet Spot for dessert.

After the food had been devoured and the dishes cleared away, Ryan and Harper were packing up Oliver's scattered toys when Coco went tearing across the lawn, barking like the watchdog she aspired to be, halting only when she ran out of leash.

Glancing up, he saw a young woman standing on the path, just out of the dog's reach. Something about her niggled at the back of Ryan's mind.

Twentysomething. Long straight dark hair, blue eyes. A little mole at the corner of her mouth. That was how Nathan had described the woman who'd been asking about a scholarship program that Garrett Furniture didn't have.

Nina or Nora…something like that. He'd forgotten her name. Truthfully, he'd forgotten about that entire conversation until now.

Now that same woman was here, and the delicious meal he'd recently enjoyed churned in his stomach. Especially when his mother drew in a breath, and his father went perfectly still.

Justin was the first to move. He met her in the middle of the yard. "Can I help you?"

"I'm looking for John Garrett."

"Why?"

"It's Father's Day." She folded her arms over her chest and faced him—all of them—her tone as defiant as her posture. "I'm here to see my father."

It was more than an hour later before Harper and Ryan left his parents' house. Nora Reardon—who turned out to be John's illegitimate daughter from a long-ago affair—hadn't stayed long. Just long enough to make her claim and unleash chaos.

They didn't talk about it on the way home. Harper could tell that Ryan was upset and she suspected that he needed some time to absorb everything he'd learned.

It wasn't until Oliver was settled and Coco was curled up beneath his crib that she finally asked him if he was okay.

"I'll let you know when my head stops spinning."

She reached for his hand, squeezed gently.

"I just never expected…anything like this," he admitted. "I always thought my parents had one of those rare committed relationships. They've been married forty-four years—I looked to them as an example of how to do things right. And I knew that when I got married, I wanted a partnership like theirs. Now I find out it's a sham."

"It's not," Harper told him. "As your mother explained it, they went through a rough patch, but they got through it. And they're still together now because they love each other."

"My father cheated on my mother." The words were blunt, but she heard the hurt and anger in his voice.

She nodded, unwilling to defend his father's infidelity. On the other hand, she had to give John credit for being honest about his actions—and the repercussions—and to both of Ryan's parents for making the effort to save their marriage notwithstanding the affair. Unlike her own parents, who were always so quick and eager to throw in the towel, divorcing and remarrying almost on a whim.

"I don't know the details of how or why—and I don't want to know," she assured him. "All I'm going to say is that your mother's obviously forgiven him, so maybe you can, too."

"She's known about his affair for more than twenty years, and she never said a word about it to any of us."

"Why would she?"

He scowled at that.

"It wasn't about you or Justin or Braden," she said gently.

"How about my half sister?" he challenged. "Was it about her?"

She suspected that he might have been able to forgive his father the indiscretion if it had been only that—a longago fling that was over and forgotten. But the knowledge that John had fathered another child was, understandably, giving him more difficulty.

"Your mother didn't know about her—and neither did your father until very recently."

"And he still didn't say a word."

"I'm sure it was a shock to him, too," she explained. "He probably needed some time to sort out his own feelings before he could talk about it."

Ryan was obviously struggling to do the same. "I can't get my head around the fact that I have a sister."

"You must be a little curious about her."

"I am. And I feel guilty about being curious."

"Because of your mom," she guessed.

"Yeah." He shook his head. "I don't want to believe it—I never would have suspected that my father was capable of such a thing. And he keeps saying 'It was a long time ago,' as if that makes it okay, but all it tells me is that I was only a few years older than Oliver is right now when my dad was screwing around on my mom."

She didn't know what to say, how to make everything okay for him. Because she hadn't grown up with even the illusion of parents who were happily married, she didn't know what it was like to have it taken away. "I was three when my mom found out my dad was sleeping with his costar," she confided to him now.

He seemed startled by this revelation. "You remember that?"

"No—but my mom likes to remind me of the fact every time she's mad at my dad."

"Is that why they split?"

She nodded. "But then they got back together again… and split up again." And while she didn't like airing dirty laundry in public—her parents did enough of that—Ryan was hardly "public" and she thought he might appreciate the focus being shifted away from his own family, at least for a minute. "And in between their three weddings and two divorces, there have been numerous other affairs— probably on both sides. Of course, because my father is moderately famous, every one of his indiscretions was front-page news for the tabloids."

"That must have sucked."

"I lost my best friend in seventh grade when her mom slept with my dad."

He winced. "How did you find out about that affair?"

"My mother told me."

Ryan looked horrified. "Does your mother have no sense of boundaries?"

"None," she confirmed.

"It's a wonder that you even considered getting married," he noted.

"I did it for Oliver."

He nodded. "I know."

Something in his tone made her feel as if she'd somehow added to his burden, which was the opposite of her intention.

"Maybe we should talk about something else," he suggested.

"Sure," she agreed. "But not talking about this isn't going to stop you thinking about it."

"I'm pretty sure that kissing you would stop me from thinking about it," he said, drawing her into his arms. "In fact, I'm pretty sure that kissing you would stop me from thinking about everything else."

She lifted her arms to his shoulders. "Then let's see what we can do to—"

The ringing of the telephone interrupted what she was saying.

"Ignore it," he suggested.

She wanted to, but a quick glance at the display revealed their lawyer's name.

"It's Shelly," she told him.

He let her go.

"I'm sorry to intrude on your weekend," Shelly said when Harper picked up the receiver. "But I just got a call from Justice Falconi's clerk. He had another trial scheduled to start Monday morning but the parties reached a settlement, so we're up."

"Monday," she echoed, looking over at Ryan, a new kind of tension seeping into the room.

"Tomorrow," Shelly confirmed. "Ten a.m."

Ten days later, Harper sat at a table beside Ryan with Shelly on the other side of him. Aubrey and Jeremy were on the other side of the courtroom with their attorney. As they waited for the judge, Harper was torn between relief that the whole ordeal was almost over and panic that a final decision was imminent. She and Ryan had done everything they could to convince the judge that it was in Oliver's best interests to remain with the guardians his parents had chosen for him. She fervently hoped their everything was enough. If they failed, they could lose custody of him forever.

At two o'clock, the clerk ordered all to rise and Justice Falconi swept into the courtroom to take his seat upon the dais.

Beneath the table, Ryan reached over and took one of her hands, linking their fingers together. She appreciated his efforts at reassurance, especially because his hands were as unsteady as her own, proving that he was as nervous as she was.

She glanced over her shoulder to confirm that Oliver was still sitting contentedly with Ryan's mother and father. The little boy had recently learned to say "Ga-ma" and Ellen Garrett was over the moon. Harper knew she'd be as devastated as anyone if the judge ruled against them. In only a few minutes, the small courtroom had started to fill as more of Ryan's family members came into the gallery to hear the judge's ruling: David and Jane, Thomas and Susan, Daniel, Kenna and Jacob, Nate and Allison, Andrew and Rachel, Tristyn, and even Justin—likely straight from the hospital, considering the scrubs that he wore. It was an impressive show of support and family solidarity, and Harper was incredibly grateful to all of them.

Looking across the courtroom at the other table, she saw that Aubrey had her head down and was chewing on a thumbnail while Jeremy stared straight ahead, his expression unreadable. Harper wasn't sure how she felt—definitely scared and frustrated that they couldn't have worked out some kind of arrangement to avoid this nasty custody battle. She would have been happy to welcome Darren's sister and her husband into their nephew's life—in fact, she and Ryan had done so. She wasn't sure that Aubrey and Jeremy would extend the same courtesy if the judge ruled in their favor—and Harper felt sick at the possibility that they could be cut right out of Oliver's life.

Unshed tears burned her eyes and clogged her throat as the judge's voice droned in the background. She tried to focus on his words as he recited the basic facts of the case and summarized the evidence presented, but her heart hurt and her thoughts were jumbled.

Ryan's fingers tightened on hers, focusing her attention back on the proceedings as Justice Falconi paused to sip from a glass of water.

He set the glass down again. "After careful consideration of the evidence presented by all parties, including the report and testimony of the minor child's guardian *ad litem*, who recommended that an orphaned child should be placed with family if at all possible, it is apparent to me that the child *is* in the care of his family. The respondents have proved that they are committed to his well-being and best interests and that their affection is not dependent on blood ties but is the result of a bond that has been building and strengthening since the birth of the child.

"I therefore confirm the interim order of Justice Burchell and hereby grant full physical and legal custody of the minor child, Oliver Darren Cannon, to the respondents, Ryan Garrett and Harper Ross-Garrett."

Harper looked past Ryan to their attorney, as if for confirmation that she'd heard the judge correctly. Shelly confirmed her unspoken question with a short nod, her attention focused on the judge, who was still speaking.

"In addition, I find that this application was if not frivolous, at least ill-advised, and I order the applicants, Jeremy Renforth and Aubrey Renforth, to pay the costs of the respondents in this matter."

Shelly stood up to thank the judge for his ruling. Opposing counsel did the same while Jeremy Renforth consoled his wife, who was sobbing.

The clerk commanded all to rise and Justice Falconi stood up. Out of the corner of her eye, Harper saw Ellen kiss the top of Oliver's head and John put his arms around both of them, hugging them tight. Somehow sensing the importance of the occasion, Oliver clapped his hands together, causing the judge to pause to look out into the gallery. The stern-faced man smiled at the little boy, then nodded and continued to his chambers.

Chapter Fifteen

"I don't think I'm ever going to get used to that alarm going off at four forty-five a.m.," Ryan grumbled as Harper reached out to silence the beeping.

She brushed her lips to his lightly. "Go back to sleep."

The words were barely out of her mouth when she realized that he already had. Unfortunately, she didn't have the same option.

Their schedules being what they were, it was only on weekends that they were able to linger in bed together—and then only if Oliver decided to sleep in a little. But after today's show, *Coffee Time with Caroline* was going on hiatus, which meant no 5:00 a.m. alarm for two full glorious weeks.

She peeked in on Oliver, as she did every morning, and smiled when she saw him sleeping peacefully. There was evidence of both Melissa and Darren in the little boy they'd made together, and she found comfort in the knowledge that they lived on through their son.

Harper was a wife and a mother now—two titles that

six months earlier she could not have imagined being applied to her. She would always regret that it had taken the loss of two of her best friends to get her to where she was now, but she loved her life with Ryan and Oliver. She loved being part of Ryan's family and the family that they'd built around Oliver.

She still wanted to make executive producer someday, but it wasn't the entire focus of her life anymore. For so long, she'd fixated on her career because it was the only thing she had. Now she had a husband and a child, and she looked forward to every day with both of them.

After the show, Harper was finalizing some details for their first week back after the holiday when Diya poked her head around the corner.

"Call for you on line one."

It wasn't the words but the excitement in her assistant's voice that made Harper ask, "Who is it?"

"Annette Grantham."

The name sounded familiar but she wasn't sure why.

Diya filled in the blanks for her. "Senior vice president of development at WMBT."

Harper picked up the receiver. Her assistant, obviously understanding the potential significance of the call, gave her two thumbs-up and closed the door.

She pressed line one. "Harper Ross. Garrett," she added, wondering how long it would take for her to get used to the new name.

"Harper—it's Annette Grantham from WMBT in Florida."

She twisted the phone cord around her hand. "What can I do for you, Ms. Grantham?"

"Come to the station for an interview," she said bluntly. "We're losing Jay Corrigan to *Sunrise in Seattle* and I don't have anyone here who can step into his shoes. I think you can."

"I'm…flattered," she said, because it sounded less obsequious than flabbergasted or ecstatic—both of which were equally true.

"Don't be," Annette said. "I'm not in the business of stroking egos. I have contacts in television all across the country, and I consider Adam McCready a personal friend. This phone call could jeopardize that friendship if I succeed in luring you away, but that's a chance I have to take. Are you interested?"

"I'm interested," Harper confirmed.

"When can you get here?"

"As of Monday, we're on hiatus for two weeks—"

"Monday works," the producer said. "Why don't we say ten a.m.?"

Her head was spinning. She had to talk to Ryan. She had to talk to Adam. She knew that going to Miami for an interview wasn't a guarantee of anything, regardless of what Ms. Grantham thought she knew or wanted, but this was the opportunity Harper had been working for and there was no way she was going to turn it down.

"I'll be there," she confirmed.

Harper went directly to Garrett Furniture when she left the studio. It seemed strange to think that she'd never been to her husband's office—but she'd never before had a reason to seek him out there. But the news about her interview in Miami was bubbling up inside her, refusing to wait until he got home.

She gave her name at reception—this time remembering to add *Garrett*—and the young woman at the desk gave directions to his office, explaining that Ryan's secretary had just gone out on lunch, so she could go right in.

His name was on the door and the L-shaped desk was offset from the opening. He was working at his computer, set up on the wall side, so he didn't see her until she was standing in front of his desk. He glanced up, a surprised—and partly guilty—smile creasing his face.

"Hard at work, I see," she noted, her gaze shifting to the picturesque beach scene that filled his monitor—a young couple embracing on a beach of white sand contrasted by crystal clear turquoise water.

"Now you've ruined the surprise," he told her.

"What surprise?"

"Our honeymoon."

She was stunned, sincerely touched and more than a little scared. Because like the wearing of his mother's veil had made her a real bride, the promise of a honeymoon seemed to make their marriage more real.

"Since we didn't know what was happening with the custody hearing when we got married, we didn't have a chance to get away," he explained. "Now that that situation is finally settled, I thought we could take a few days."

"The custody hearing is why we got married," she reminded him.

"One of the reasons," he agreed. "So where would you like to go? I know it's short notice, but I figured we could squeeze in a trip while *Coffee Time* is on hiatus. With or without Oliver—your choice. But I have to tell you, my mom is pushing for us to leave the little guy with her."

It was an incredibly romantic gesture, and the idea of spending a few days on a beach somewhere with Ryan was undeniably tempting. Almost tempting enough to make her forget that she'd already committed to being in Miami the following week.

"Actually, I have to be in Florida on Monday," she told him.

"Why?"

"I got a call from Annette Grantham at WMBT. She's looking for a new executive producer for *Mid-Day Miami* and wants to interview me."

"When's the interview?"

"Ten a.m. Monday morning."

"Miami isn't Jamaica," he said. "But that could work."

She shook her head. "It's a job interview, not a vacation."

"There's no reason we couldn't spend a few days at the beach after the interview," he said.

"Having you there might be too much of a distraction."

"Then I'll come Monday night."

It sounded perfectly reasonable, but Harper wasn't feeling reasonable. The call had been unexpected and so were the emotions churning inside her. This was what she'd wanted for so long, and now that she was on the cusp of getting what she'd wanted, she was feeling torn. Because as much as she wanted the job, she didn't want to leave Ryan and Oliver—even for a few days. And the unexpected offer to go with her only added to Harper's confusion.

"I don't need you there." She'd worked hard to get where she was in her career, and she'd done it on her own. His unexpected show of support didn't just surprise her—it worried her, as if sharing any part of this trip with him would somehow make the opportunity less than her own. She knew it didn't make sense, but it was how she felt.

She didn't need him there, but there was a part of her— maybe the biggest part—that did *want* him there. And the wanting scared her. She couldn't let herself rely on him, because then she'd be lost without him when he was gone.

She looked at the rings on her finger, the beautiful diamond solitaire he'd given to her the day he asked her to marry him and the matching band he'd slid on her finger when he promised to love, honor and cherish her. She'd spoken the same words to him, wanting to believe that their marriage would last forever but not really trusting that it could.

"I know you don't need me there," he said patiently. "I was hoping you'd want me there. It doesn't seem unreasonable to me that you'd discuss a major career relocation with your husband before you make a final decision."

Somehow those words were what she needed—his pointed reminder of their marital status gave her a target for all of her conflicted emotions. "I'm not giving up this opportunity just because I'm wearing your ring on my finger."

He drew back to look at her, his gaze intent—and showing a hint of frustration. "Do you think I would ask you to?"

"I don't know," she admitted.

"If that's true, then you don't know me at all."

"Maybe I don't," she allowed. "Everything happened so fast—too fast. I know we were both trying to do what was best for Oliver, but maybe playing at being a family—"

"Is that what you think this is?" he interjected, his tone moving beyond frustration to anger now. "Some kind of elaborate make-believe?"

He wasn't just angry, she realized—he was hurt, and she was sorry for that, but she couldn't back down. "Isn't it?"

"No. Our marriage is real. Our *family* is real. My *feelings* for you are *real*, dammit. I love you!" Then he drew in a breath and said it again, not yelling or swearing at her this time. "I love you, Harper."

She sat down, hard. Her knees felt like jelly. Her heart was pounding so hard and fast inside her chest she felt as if her ribs might crack. She wanted to believe him—she so desperately wanted to believe him! But she was wary. This was a man who had manipulated her into marriage to bolster their claim for custody. How could she be sure that he wasn't using those words to manipulate her emotions to his own purposes now? The truth was, she couldn't.

He was silent, watching her, obviously waiting for some kind of response.

"Your timing sucks," she told him.

One side of his mouth turned up a little. "I know. And my delivery could use some work, too." He sat down beside her and took her hands in his. "But neither of those factors makes my feelings any less real."

Her throat was tight and her eyes burned. She knew he wanted her to say the words back to him, but she couldn't. Because the truth was, she wasn't sure how she felt. When she was with him, she felt as if she was finally where she belonged. But how much of that was directly linked to their desire to give Oliver the real family he'd lost when his parents were killed? The past few months had been such an emotional roller coaster that she honestly didn't know.

"Our lives have been in complete turmoil the past several months," she pointed out to him. "It's been a long and difficult journey and I'm so grateful that you were by my side through all of the highs and lows."

"You're…grateful?"

"I am," she insisted, struggling to find the right words to explain. "I don't know that I could have gotten through any of it on my own. But I can't help but wonder if what we feel for one another would have developed outside this situation or if everything is tied up in our emotional connection to Oliver."

"You think I don't know what's in my own heart?"

"I'm not sure I know what's in mine," she told him. "But I hope this trip to Miami will give me the time and space I need to figure it out."

"When are you leaving?"

"I thought I'd fly out on Sunday."

"Why wait?" he said. "If you need time and space, why not go today?"

She understood then how much she'd hurt him. Not on purpose, of course, but the lack of intent didn't mitigate the result. She didn't want to leave like this, but even if she stayed a few more days and tried to set things right, what purpose would that serve? It wasn't as if she had any intention of changing her plans. She was still going to get on a plane to Miami to participate in the interview that had been offered to her.

After that... Well, she'd figure that out after. For now they'd said everything they needed to say—and maybe more than they should have.

"I'll pick Oliver up on the way home," she said.

"Fine."

She glanced at the computer screen, at the white sand and turquoise water, and wondered if that might be the closest she would ever get to a honeymoon with her husband.

By the time Ryan got home from the office, Harper had her flight booked and her suitcase packed.

"I guess you decided not to wait."

She looked at him, hurt and confusion and maybe a little bit of regret in her eyes. "You told me to go."

"Yeah, I did," he acknowledged. "I just didn't anticipate that you'd finally listen to something I said."

"A few days apart will be good for us."

He didn't agree, but it was obvious that she'd made up her mind, so he only asked, "When will you be back?"

"After my interview."

"Okay."

Oliver had been playing on the floor with his blocks;

Coco was beside him chewing on a rope. She picked up the little boy and gave him a big hug and kiss. "Auntie Harper has to go bye-bye for a few days."

Oliver curled his fingers down to his palm, waving. "Bye-bye."

"You be a good boy for Uncle Ryan while I'm gone, okay?"

"Bye-bye."

She smiled, then pressed her lips together when they trembled as she put Oliver back in the middle of his blocks.

"Can you text me your flight details?" he asked her.

She nodded. "Sure."

He caught her hand as she reached the door, halting her departure just long enough to kiss her. He was mad and he was hurt, but he couldn't let her leave with harsh words being the last thing they exchanged.

She kissed him back, and when he finally let her go, there were tears in her eyes. Without another word, she walked out.

Oliver toddled over to where Ryan stood at the window, watching as the taxi that carried Harper away from them backed out of the driveway. He lifted his hand and waved again. "Bye-bye."

Ryan watched until the vehicle was out of view, wondering if he'd done the right thing—letting her go. Not that he could have made her stay, but he could have gone with her. Of course, he still could, but she'd made it clear that this was something she wanted and needed to do on her own. Which meant that he had to let her—for better or for worse. But as he turned away from the window, he felt as if his heart was a lead weight inside his chest.

He picked up Oliver and propped him on his hip. "Well, it looks like it's just you and me, kid. So what should we do tonight—smoke cigars, drink beer and play poker?"

"Po-ka."

"Sounds good to me," Ryan said. "But maybe we should swap the cigars and beer for spaghetti and milk?"

"Um," Oliver agreed.

Spending the weekend in Miami sounded great in theory but was incredibly lonely in reality.

Harper checked into her hotel, worked out in the gym, swam in the pool and watched a lot of WMBT. And she missed Ryan and Oliver—every minute of every day.

On Sunday morning, she decided to track down an old friend who had moved to the Sunshine State a few years earlier. Paige was living in West Palm Beach now but was happy to make the trip to Miami to have dinner with Harper.

They exchanged pleasantries, then talked a little bit about Harper's upcoming interview and Paige's work as an interior designer for the rich and outrageous.

"And what's Jim doing now?" she asked, naming her friend's husband.

"He's managing a resort in Naples."

"Isn't that on the other side of the state?"

Paige nodded. "He moved there after the divorce, almost three years ago."

"I'm sorry—I didn't realize you weren't together anymore."

Her friend shrugged. "It wasn't a particularly acrimonious split. It just turned out that, after five years together, we realized we didn't even like one another all that much."

While Harper was glad that Paige wasn't torn up over the demise of her marriage, it seemed sad to her that a couple who had exchanged vows could walk away from one another so easily. Sad but not really surprising, since it demonstrated a cavalier attitude similar to that demonstrated by her own parents.

Maybe that was why when Ryan suggested marriage to strengthen their case for permanent custody of Oliver, she hadn't really balked at the concept. Their marriage had been entered into for a specific purpose and without any illusions about happy-ever-after. If the marriage stopped working, for whatever reason, she expected they would simply part ways.

It was only now that she realized she didn't want a temporary marriage—she wanted a forever family, like Ryan's family. And she wanted Ryan and Oliver to be part of that forever family.

When she got back to her hotel later that night, she tried to focus on the interview that was scheduled for the following morning. She was excited but not worried, and while she believed she was ready for the challenges and capable of doing the job, she was no longer certain she wanted it.

She tried to sleep, because she knew she shouldn't go into the interview with shadows under her eyes, but it was too quiet. She was accustomed to hearing the sounds of Oliver rustling in his crib through the baby monitor and the steady rhythm of Ryan's breathing from the pillow beside her.

She hadn't talked to him since she'd walked out of the house Friday night. She'd texted to let him know that her flight had landed and then again when she was checked into her hotel, but she hadn't actually spoken to him since she'd left Charisma. She thought about calling, just to hear his voice, but the way they'd left things, she wasn't sure he'd want to talk to her. And she'd rather not talk to him than risk an awkward or uncomfortable conversation. At least, that was what she'd told herself when she'd been tempted to pick up the phone Friday night and again Saturday night. But now she missed him so much she was almost desperate for the sound of his voice.

She looked at the clock beside her bed. It was nearly midnight. She knew it was possible—probable, even—that he was still up, but she didn't want to call now in case he was sleeping.

She sent him a text message instead.

Just wanted to say good-night to you and Oliver. xoxo

His response came before she'd even set her phone back on the nightstand.

we miss u lots sweet dreams xoxo

It wasn't quite as good as hearing his voice, but it made her feel a little better. She put the phone aside and tried to fall asleep.

She got another text from Ryan before she left the hotel the next morning.

break a leg

Short and simple, but somehow Harper knew that those three words represented so much more. It wasn't just that he was wishing her luck—it was confirmation that he wanted her to succeed because it was what she wanted.

He'd been nothing but supportive of her career, and she realized now how completely unfair it had been to suggest that he wouldn't want her to pursue this opportunity. It had been equally unfair to make her plans without talking to him first. She'd been so focused on her own wants she hadn't considered anything else.

And while she could and did regret the way she'd handled the situation, she realized that she'd needed to take this trip without him. She'd needed the time and space away from Ryan to realize how much she didn't want to be away from him.

She walked into WMBT on Monday morning confident that she'd done her research on both the station and its head. The website photo showed Annette Grantham to be a serious-looking woman with short dark hair, intense blue eyes and a firm, unsmiling mouth. She'd worked in television for thirty-four years, had received numerous industry awards and been nominated for countless more.

In person she was just as serious and direct—and a lot shorter than Harper had expected. About five-three, she guessed, with lots of energy packed into her compact body. She walked fast and talked even faster through a quick tour of the studio. She knew the names of every single studio employee, from casting directors to key grips to janitorial staff. But even more impressive was the obvious respect that each of those employees had for her.

The more time Harper spent there, the more her interest was piqued. *Mid-Day Miami* was a high-profile show offering a significant increase in salary commensurate with a new title and responsibilities and a production schedule that wouldn't require her to get out of bed when the sky was still dark.

It was everything that she wanted—except that it was in Miami and Ryan and Oliver were in Charisma.

If the job was offered and Harper turned it down, she could wait years before she saw another similar opportunity—if she ever did. But the thought of spending even a single day of those years without her husband and the little boy they both loved... She couldn't do it. She didn't want to do it.

She shook Annette Grantham's hand and thanked her for her time.

"I'll be in touch before the end of the week," the senior VP of development promised.

"I'll look forward to hearing from you."

It wasn't yet eleven o'clock when Harper walked out of the building, but the Florida sun was high in the sky and the air was already hot and sticky. She was looking forward to the return flight to Charisma with a much lighter heart than the one that had come here. Because she knew without a doubt now that she was in love with her husband, and at the very first opportunity, she was going to tell him so.

Chapter Sixteen

Harper intended to call Ryan from the airport, to tell him that she was on her way home, but he called her first.

She suspected that he wanted to hear about her interview and was surprised when he didn't even mention the purpose for her trip to Florida. Instead, he said, "I don't want you to worry," which, of course, immediately caused her to worry.

"What's wrong?"

"There was a situation at the day care."

"Is Oliver hurt?"

"No, he's fine. But Aubrey showed up there today and told the supervisor that you'd sent her to pick him up."

"Ohmygod." Harper's knees buckled and she sank into an empty chair inside the departure lounge, her heart pounding and her head spinning. "They didn't let her take him, did they?"

"No," he hastened to assure her. "Because she wasn't on the approved list, they called me to ask if it was okay."

She felt sick to her stomach thinking about what could have happened if the day care had released Oliver to Aubrey. Would she have run away with him? Taken him to another country to live under an assumed name? She knew the possibility was far-fetched, but it did happen.

Harper pressed a hand to her churning stomach. She'd found Aubrey's determination to gain custody of her nephew a little extreme, but she'd trusted that the woman would abide by the judge's ruling. The possibility that she might try to take Oliver against the explicit orders of the court had never crossed her mind.

"Is Oliver with you now?"

"I'm less than ten minutes from the day care," he told her.

She was grateful that he was, because she was in Florida, eight hundred miles away. She was suddenly and painfully aware of the distance, and she felt completely helpless and terrified.

"I'll call you back in a little while so you can talk to Oliver," Ryan suggested.

In the background, she heard the gate agent announce the start of boarding. "I'm going to be on a plane in a few minutes," she told him.

Harper felt marginally better after talking to Ryan.

When she was buckled into her seat on the plane, she texted him her flight information and estimated time of arrival at home. He didn't reply. She kept her cell in her hand, waiting, hoping, for a response, but there was nothing. Her throat was tight as she set her phone to airplane mode, knowing that every minute that she was out of touch was going to feel like an hour, that the two-hour flight would feel like forever.

Unable to receive any communications from Ryan, she

tried to console herself with the reassurance that he'd gone to the day care as he'd promised and Oliver was safe with him by now. But she really needed to see him for herself. She needed to see both of them.

She checked her phone again for a message as she left the Jetway, and her gaze was so intently focused on the screen of her phone that she nearly walked right past them in the arrivals area. Then she heard her name and she looked up—and saw them.

Ryan and Oliver.

Here.

Real.

Safe.

She couldn't speak. There were no words—there was only emotion. A huge overwhelming wave of emotion— gratitude, relief, joy—that swept over her.

Then Ryan's arms were around her, warm and strong, holding her close for a long time.

"You didn't text me back," she finally managed, the words muffled against his chest.

"I forgot my phone in the car when I went in to get Oliver," he admitted. "And by the time we left the day care, I knew your plane was already in the air and decided you wouldn't believe that he was safe until you saw him for yourself."

"You're right," she admitted.

"And he is—safe and secure and where he belongs. With us."

Oliver was also sandwiched between them, and he began to squirm against the constraint of their embrace. Ryan reluctantly let go of her and shifted the little boy to her arms.

She hugged Oliver close and kissed the top of his head, while Ryan stroked a hand over her hair, as if he needed the physical contact to prove to himself that she was there. She understood the feeling.

"Can we go home now?" she asked.

"Whenever you're ready."

Home was chaos.

Oliver had fallen asleep in the car but woke up as soon as Ryan pulled into the driveway. Then Coco went nuts when they walked through the door, dancing around between their feet and yipping happily.

"Is it good to be home?" Ryan asked.

She smiled. "You have no idea how good."

They took the baby and the puppy out into the yard and let them run around to burn off some energy. Ryan dropped onto the grass and pulled her down beside him. She was still wearing the linen pantsuit she'd donned for her interview with Annette Grantham a lifetime ago, and she knew that she'd end up with grass stains on the butt, but she didn't care.

She tipped her head back against Ryan's shoulder and smiled, watching Oliver chase Coco for a few steps; then Coco would turn around and chase Oliver. And in that moment, her life was pretty much perfect.

"I didn't even ask," Harper realized. "What happened with Aubrey? Was she arrested?"

"The day-care manager called the police, but they said it was our choice whether or not to have her charged," Ryan told her.

"And you opted not," she guessed.

"I said I'd have to discuss it with you, but Aubrey's attorney pointed out that there's no evidence she wanted to take Oliver from the day care for any reason other than a visit."

She snorted her disbelief.

"That was my reaction, too," he said. "But the attorney also suggested that his clients might agree to a stipulation of supervised visitation if we chose not to pursue other legal remedies."

"I don't know that pressing charges would accomplish anything," she said. "At least that's something."

"There's something else," Ryan said, and pulled Oliver's beanbag puppy out of his pocket.

"You found Woof."

"Aubrey found Woof."

"She must have been at the cemetery on Mother's Day, after we left," Harper realized.

"And at the courthouse when we got married," Ryan said.

"What?"

So he told her about Oliver "finding" the toy that day—and how he'd thrown it away. And now it had turned up again, courtesy of Aubrey.

"That's a little scary," Harper said.

He didn't disagree.

Then Oliver plopped himself on the ground beside them and looked at Harper hopefully. "Kee?"

She chuckled. "Are you hungry?"

"Kee," he said again.

"I guess it's getting close to dinnertime," Ryan realized.

Her stomach growled in agreement, the bowl of fruit and yogurt she'd had at breakfast nothing more than a distant memory.

"I had big plans for a special meal for your first night home," he told her. "Spaghetti Bolognese, garlic bread sticks and salad, of course."

"Takeout from Valentino's?" she guessed.

"Yeah. How does that sound?"

"Delicious," she admitted. "But too much trouble."

"Too much trouble to go pick it up?"

She nodded. "I don't want you to go anywhere right now."

"We could get pizza delivered."

"Za," Oliver chimed in.

"Za sounds even better," she agreed, ruffling the little boy's hair.

"There won't be any salad," Ryan warned.

"We could get tomatoes and green peppers on the pizza."

"We could," he agreed. "But we won't."

"Spinach and mushrooms?" she suggested.

"How about pepperoni, sausage and bacon?" he countered.

She made a face.

In the end, they compromised on pepperoni, mushrooms and hot peppers. They had a glass of wine with their pizza—a bottle of Harper's favorite cab merlot that Ryan had picked up as part of his original dinner plan.

After the pizza box was empty, Oliver had been bathed and tucked into his crib, and the puppy had settled into his own bed for the night, Ryan framed her face with his hands and kissed her softly. "I missed you."

"I missed you, too," she admitted.

"How was your interview this morning?"

"Was it only this morning?"

He smiled. "It's been a helluva day, hasn't it?"

"Not one I ever want to repeat," she assured him.

"The interview," he prompted.

"I think it went well. Annette said she'd be in touch before the end of the week."

"For a second interview or an offer?"

She shrugged. "It doesn't matter."

"What do you mean—it doesn't matter?"

"Even if she offered me the job, I wouldn't take it."

"Why not?" he demanded.

"Because it's in Miami."

"And?" he prompted.

"And…you're here. You and Oliver and Coco."

"I offered to go to Miami with you," he reminded her.

"For the interview," she acknowledged.

"For anything you need."

Her brow furrowed. "I'm not sure I understand."

"This is the opportunity you've been working toward—if you need to go to Miami to make it happen, then we'll go to Miami."

"Just like that?"

"Do you want me to make it difficult?"

"Of course not. But what about your career?"

"I'm the national sales manager of Garrett Furniture. My office is in Charisma because I'm here, but I could do the job from almost anywhere."

"What about Oliver?"

He paused, as if considering the question. "We should probably take him with us," he finally decided. "And Coco, too."

She rolled her eyes. "I was asking if you think Darren and Melissa would approve of us taking Oliver to Florida."

"They trusted us to do what's best for their son," he reminded her. "And I'm certain they wouldn't care where we're living so long as we're together."

"You'd really move to Florida?"

"It's better than either of the alternatives—you giving up a job you really want or living apart from you."

"They haven't actually offered me the job yet."

"They will," he said confidently. "And I wanted to be prepared for when they did, which is why I've already talked to the board of directors about relocating."

"Is your mother on the board of directors?"

He laughed softly. "No, but she'll understand."

Harper wasn't entirely convinced of that, but she had a more important question to ask. "Why?"

"Why do I want to do this?"

She nodded.

"Because I know this is important to you, and because you're important to me. Because I love you."

And she was finally beginning to believe that he did. "You mentioned that…before I left for Miami. And I didn't say anything back."

"Actually, you did—you said my timing sucked," he reminded her.

"I was scared," she admitted. "Because I thought you were using your feelings to manipulate me, because I didn't know what to do with all of the feelings that I had inside me."

"Are you still scared?"

"No." She looked into his eyes, wanting him to see the truth of her feelings in hers. "Because I know now that I love you, too." Then she leaned forward and kissed him, softly, sweetly. "For now and forever."

* * * * *

Don't miss the next installment of
THOSE ENGAGING GARRETTS!
by award-winning author Brenda Harlen!

*Garrett Furniture heiress Jordyn Garrett doesn't
believe in happily-ever-after—no matter what her
love-struck relatives tell her! Can sexy bartender Marco
Palermo convince her that some people are destined to
be together—and that forever is the right path for them?*

*Look for THE BACHELOR TAKES A BRIDE,
on sale September 2015, wherever Harlequin books
and ebooks are sold.*

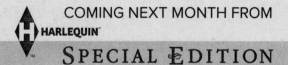

COMING NEXT MONTH FROM

HARLEQUIN®

SPECIAL EDITION

Available May 19, 2015

#2407 FORTUNE'S JUNE BRIDE
The Fortunes of Texas: Cowboy Country • by Allison Leigh
Galen Fortune Jones isn't the marrying kind...until he's roped into playing groom at the new Cowboy Country theme park in Horseback Hollow, Texas. His "bride," beautiful Aurora McElroy, piques his interest, especially when she needs a real-life fake husband. This one cowboy may have just met his match!

#2408 THE PRINCESS AND THE SINGLE DAD
Royal Babies • by Leanne Banks
Princess Sasha of Sergenia fled her dangerous home country for the principality of Chantaine. There, she assumes another identity: nanny to handsome construction specialist Gavin Sinclair's two adorable children. As the princess falls hard for the proud papa, can she form a royal family of her very own?

#2409 HER RED-CARPET ROMANCE
Matchmaking Mamas • by Marie Ferrarella
Film producer Lukas Spader needs to get his work life in order, so he hires professional organizer Yohanna Andrzejewski. She's temptingly beautiful, but Lukas must keep his eyes on his job, not his stunning new employee. As Cupid's arrow strikes them both, though, Yohanna might just fix her sexy boss's life into a happily-ever-after!

#2410 THE INSTANT FAMILY MAN
The Barlow Brothers • by Shirley Jump
Luke Barlow is happily living the single life in Stone Gap, North Carolina—until his ex's gorgeous little sister, Peyton Reynolds, shows up. She announces Luke is now the caretaker for a four-year-old daughter he never knew about. Determined to be a good dad, Luke tries to create a home for little Maddy and her aunt, one that might just be for forever...

#2411 DYLAN'S DADDY DILEMMA
The Colorado Fosters • by Tracy Madison
Chelsea Bell needs help--fast. The single mom has landed in Steamboat Springs, Colorado, and is out of money. So when dashing Dylan Foster offers her and her son, Henry, a place to stay, Chelsea's floored. Why would a complete stranger offer her help, let alone bond with her little boy? This is just the first surprise in store for one unexpected family.

#2412 FALLING FOR THE MOM-TO-BE
Home in Heartlandia • by Lynne Marshall
Ever since his wife passed away, Leif Andersen has had no time for love. Enter Marta Hoyas, a beautiful—and *pregnant!*—artist who's in town to paint a local mural. She's also living in Leif's house while she does so. The last thing Marta wants is to fall for someone who couldn't be a father to her unborn child, but Leif might just be the perfect dad-to-be.

HSECNM0515

REQUEST YOUR FREE BOOKS!

2 FREE NOVELS PLUS 2 FREE GIFTS!

Ⓗ HARLEQUIN®

SPECIAL EDITION

Life, Love & Family

YES! Please send me 2 FREE Harlequin® Special Edition novels and my 2 FREE gifts (gifts are worth about $10). After receiving them, if I don't wish to receive any more books, I can return the shipping statement marked "cancel." If I don't cancel, I will receive 6 brand-new novels every month and be billed just $4.74 per book in the U.S. or $5.49 per book in Canada. That's a savings of at least 12% off the cover price! It's quite a bargain! Shipping and handling is just 50¢ per book in the U.S. and 75¢ per book in Canada.* I understand that accepting the 2 free books and gifts places me under no obligation to buy anything. I can always return a shipment and cancel at any time. Even if I never buy another book, the two free books and gifts are mine to keep forever.

235/335 HDN GH3Z

Name	(PLEASE PRINT)	
Address		Apt. #
City	State/Prov.	Zip/Postal Code

Signature (if under 18, a parent or guardian must sign)

Mail to the **Reader Service:**
IN U.S.A.: P.O. Box 1867, Buffalo, NY 14240-1867
IN CANADA: P.O. Box 609, Fort Erie, Ontario L2A 5X3

Want to try two free books from another line?
Call 1-800-873-8635 or visit www.ReaderService.com.

* Terms and prices subject to change without notice. Prices do not include applicable taxes. Sales tax applicable in N.Y. Canadian residents will be charged applicable taxes. Offer not valid in Quebec. This offer is limited to one order per household. Not valid for current subscribers to Harlequin Special Edition books. All orders subject to credit approval. Credit or debit balances in a customer's account(s) may be offset by any other outstanding balance owed by or to the customer. Please allow 4 to 6 weeks for delivery. Offer available while quantities last.

Your Privacy—The Reader Service is committed to protecting your privacy. Our Privacy Policy is available online at www.ReaderService.com or upon request from the Reader Service.

We make a portion of our mailing list available to reputable third parties that offer products we believe may interest you. If you prefer that we not exchange your name with third parties, or if you wish to clarify or modify your communication preferences, please visit us at www.ReaderService.com/consumerschoice or write to us at Reader Service Preference Service, P.O. Box 9062, Buffalo, NY 14240-9062. Include your complete name and address.

Galen tucked the "deed" into his shirt and nudged along
his horse, Blaze, with a squeeze of his knees. He set his
white hat more firmly on his head so it wouldn't go blow-
ing off when they made their mad dash down Main. "But
I'm definitely not looking for a career change. Ranching's
in my blood. Only thing I ever wanted to do. Amusing as
this might be for now, I'll be happy as hell to hand over
Rusty's hat to whoever they get to replace Joey." He took
in the other riders as well as Cabot and gathered his reins.
"Y'all ready?"

They nodded, and as one, they set off in a thunder of
horse hooves.

Eleven minutes later on the dot, he was pulling Aurora
into his arms after "knocking" Frank off his feet, saying "I do" to Harlan's Preacher Man and bending Aurora
low over his arm while the audience—always larger on a

Saturday—clapped and hooted.

Unfortunately for Galen, the longer he'd gone without Rusty actually kissing Lila, the more he couldn't stop thinking about it as he pressed his cheek against Aurora's, her head tucked down in his chest.

"Big crowd," he whispered. The mikes were dead and he held her a little longer than usual. Because of the lengthy applause they were getting, of course.

"Too big," she whispered back. "You going to let me up anytime soon?"

He immediately straightened, and she smiled broadly at the crowd, waving her hand as she tucked her hand through his arm and they strolled offstage.

But he could see through the smile to the frustration brewing in her blue eyes.

He waited until they were well away from the stage. "Sorry about that."

"About what?" She impatiently pushed her veil behind her back and kept looking over her shoulder as they strode through the side street. She was damn near jogging, and the beads hanging from her dress were bouncing.

"Holding the…uh…the…uh…" He yanked his string tie loose, feeling like an idiot. "You know. The embrace."

She gave him a distracted look. "What about it?"

"Holding it so long."

Don't miss
FORTUNE'S JUNE BRIDE
by Allison Leigh,
available June 2015 wherever
Harlequin® Special Edition books and ebooks are sold.

www.Harlequin.com

THE WORLD IS BETTER WITH
Romance

Harlequin has everything from contemporary, passionate and heartwarming to suspenseful and inspirational stories.

Whatever your mood,
we have a romance just for you!

Connect with us to find your next great read,
special offers and more.

f /HarlequinBooks

🐦 @HarlequinBooks

www.HarlequinBlog.com

www.Harlequin.com/Newsletters